Nothing Personal

Look for these titles by
Jaci Burton

Now Available:

Rescue Me
Show Me
Unwrapped

Coming Soon:

Dare to Love
Crimson Ties

Holiday Seduction: Unwrapped
(print anthology with Lauren Dane)

Sneak Peek: Show Me
(print anthology with Shelley Bradley)

Nothing Personal

Jaci Burton

A Samhain Publishing, Ltd. publication.

Samhain Publishing, Ltd.
577 Mulberry Street, Suite 1520
Macon, GA 31201
www.samhainpublishing.com

Nothing Personal
Copyright © 2008 by Jaci Burton
Print ISBN: 978-1-60504-107-0
Digital ISBN: 1-59998-170-X

Editing by Angie James
Cover by Scott Carpenter

First Samhain Publishing, Ltd. electronic publication: March 2007
First Samhain Publishing, Ltd. print publication: June 2008

Dedication

To my editor, Angela James—you are the wind beneath my wings, the sunshine of my soul, the yin to my yang, the cream to my coffee and the butter to my toast. Okay, seriously, thank you for always knowing the difference between lay/lie/laid, affect/effect, awhile and for a while, and which of my sentences really suck, because there's only so much information my limited brain can handle.

And to Charlie—you have always made me feel valued, cherished and loved, and for that I will be forever grateful.

Chapter One

"If you think Ryan McKay's so hot, Faith, then *you* marry him."

Faith Lewis watched in stunned silence as her boss's bride-to-be flounced out of the penthouse suite, the train of her designer wedding gown trailing gloriously behind her.

No more than a moment after Erica Stanton walked out the door in a huff, Ryan McKay stepped in.

He threw Faith that look. The irritated, things-weren't-going-his-way-and-he-wasn't-happy-about-it look. The same expression crossed his handsome features at countless business meetings.

"I saw Erica leaving," he said. "I called to her, but she slipped into the elevator before I could get there."

Mere inches separated them. His six-foot frame towered over her, his crisp, clean scent calling to mind snow-covered mountain breezes. No man should be allowed to smell that good. Black hair, gray eyes and broad shoulders, he was the picture of handsome elegance. Her heart fluttered despite his angry scowl.

"Faith, what's going on?" Ryan asked.

Offering up a silent *thanks a lot* to Ryan's now-former fiancée, she braced herself to deliver the bad news. This went way beyond her job as his executive assistant. "Umm, Miss Stanton has changed her mind about marrying you."

Prepared for the inevitable McKay tirade, Faith couldn't believe the disappointment shadowing his powerful features. "I see," he said. "You couldn't convince her?"

She'd never seen that defeated look before. Ryan McKay never gave up. But he *was* quickly running out of options. He had roughly five hours to get married or lose control of McKay Corporation and it was now a certainty that Erica Stanton wasn't going to be the bride. That meant it was time to execute Plan B. She wondered if there actually was a Plan B.

"I tried, Mr. McKay, really I did. She changed her mind about having your child." Faith had tried her best, but the ice queen had refused to listen to reason. No matter what she suggested, Erica countered. Faith surmised that Erica simply didn't want to ruin her cover-girl body with a pregnancy.

"We went over that a hundred times and she assured me she could handle it." Ryan glanced at his watch, then back at Faith. "I don't understand it. I'm the CEO of McKay Corporation. The Chalet Casino Hotel is the most prominent hotel in Las Vegas and I'm a multimillionaire. So why can't I find one single woman willing to marry me?"

Faith opened her mouth to speak, then closed it. Silly thought, anyway.

"Tell me, Faith. Why the hell did I wait until the last minute when I had a year to get this done?"

She studied her sensible shoes and clasped her hands behind her back. "Actually, Mr. McKay, I...um, reminded you of that very fact several months ago."

"Yeah, yeah, I know." He sighed. "I thought I could find a loophole in Grandfather's will that would get me out of needing to marry. After wasting nearly a year, I still haven't found one."

Ryan plopped down on the sofa nearby, the Italian leather giving with a *whoosh*. He leaned his head back and closed his eyes.

She wanted to offer him comfort—wanted to sit down, pull him into her arms and reassure him. But, of course that would never happen. She wouldn't dare. They didn't have that kind of relationship. They didn't have a relationship at all. She was an employee and nothing more.

Instead, she stood next to the sofa and waited, wondering if there was something else she could have said to Erica to convince the woman to go ahead with the wedding. Certainly appealing to Erica's soft side would have done no good—she didn't have one.

Tall, blonde and nearly perfect, Erica had one fatal flaw, in Faith's opinion. She was utterly cold. Like a stone statue—a Venus of incredible beauty, but devoid of life or any emotion. Why Ryan had chosen to marry Erica was something Faith would never understand. Then again, this deal wasn't exactly a love match, so it didn't really matter who he chose as the woman he married.

But Erica? The homeless bag lady who wandered the streets would have been a warmer choice.

Ryan opened his eyes and stared at her. Faith's heart leaped. Had he heard her quiet chuckle?

His gaze held hers and warmth seeped into her middle. She'd never had a steady man in her life, but if she had a fantasy guy he would look like Ryan McKay. Hair the color of midnight and turbulent eyes like the Oklahoma storms she remembered as a child.

She'd loved those come-out-of-nowhere squalls while growing up in her small town. Whenever a storm approached, she'd run outside onto the front porch and watch as the clouds gathered momentum, moving ever closer until the wind whipped her back inside the house to watch from the safety of the windows.

The energy had always charged her. The storms shook her to the core, fired up the energy around her and took her with them in a maelstrom of fury and passion.

Ryan's eyes were like that. Changing like rolling clouds and loaded with the fire of a blistering rainstorm. She had seen those eyes flash with brilliance, light with anger, and shine like a glittering diamond when he closed a deal. Never had she seen them spark with passion, but she could imagine it.

"Faith, are you listening?"

"Oh. Oh, Mr. McKay, I'm so sorry." She shook off the daydream. How many times over the years had she fantasized about him? She thought she'd finally had a handle on her crush and could now think of him only as her boss. He was, after all, as unattainable as a man could get.

At least for her.

"I asked you to sit." He patted the sofa cushion next to him.

She sat. Clear on the opposite end.

"Faith."

"Yes?" She pulled a notepad out of her bag, ready to take down instructions.

"Come closer. You're half a mile away. I won't bite." He flashed her that charming, devastating smile that made her insides melt away. Maybe he wouldn't bite, but then again maybe she'd like him to.

Really, she had to stop her errant thoughts. Ryan was her boss. The one who never noticed her. She remembered her mother's lessons well. Not a day went by during her childhood that her mother hadn't reminded her to blend in and not call attention to herself—to stay away from men because they'd only hurt her. She was plain, her mother had told her, had little to offer and she'd better use her brains because her looks would get her nowhere in life.

She'd spent twenty-six years believing those words to be true. Every time she looked in the mirror she recalled her mother's warnings.

At Ryan's urging, she scooted a bit toward the center of the sofa, pulling her wool skirt down further over her shins. He motioned her closer. She moved. Another inch.

"This is ridiculous." Ryan closed the distance, situating next to her in the center of the sofa. Their thighs touched. Faith's burned. The room was definitely getting warm.

"I can't talk to you when you're so far away," he said. "As I said before when you clearly weren't listening, I need your help."

Desperately trying for focus, she nodded. "Of course. Anything at all I can do to assist you, you know I will."

He tilted his head, examining her with inquisitive eyes. "You're single, aren't you?"

"Yes."

"Boyfriend?"

"No."

"Involved? Dating anyone right now?"

What was this about? He never asked personal questions about her. In the five years she'd worked for him, she'd found out every minute detail of his life, from his childhood to present day. But he never once asked about hers. Why would he? And why was he asking now?

"No, not dating anyone. Not involved. Mr. McKay, may I ask why you're curious about my personal life?"

"I have a solution, but wanted to be sure I wasn't stepping on any toes first."

A rolling ache formed in the pit of her stomach. She swallowed. "A solution?"

"Yes. You know how I depend on you to help me with McKay Corporation. I need your help to hold on to it."

"What can I do?" Did she really want the answer? Some thread of an idea crept into her head, but surely Ryan wouldn't suggest it. Not with her. The very thought was ludicrous and she quickly banished it from her mind.

Ryan took the pen from her fingers and picked up her hands. Faith glanced down. Her hands looked so small encased within his. Her entire body trembled with the reaction of feeling the full-on contact of his skin against hers for the first time. Other than the brief brushing of knuckles when they passed a file back and forth, he'd never touched her. And definitely not like this.

"Marry me, Faith."

The earth stopped turning. Her mind whirled with his soft-spoken words and her heart beat a rapid rhythm that threatened to send her spiraling into oblivion. She felt sick to her stomach.

Fainting would be a bad idea right now. So would throwing up. She probably heard wrong, anyway. "Could you repeat that?"

"Marry me."

His whispered breath caressed her face. He'd asked the question she thought she'd never hear from a man. Any man. And never in her wildest dreams from Ryan McKay.

She swallowed. "You can't be serious." Her voice wasn't working, coming out in a raspy squeak that sounded nothing like her. She was certain Ryan was close enough to hear the thumping of her heart as it tried to escape her chest. Her body vibrated from her rapid breaths as she struggled to control her errant thoughts.

If she kept this up she'd soon be breathing into a paper bag.

"I'm always serious about any proposal I make. This makes perfect sense to me, and it should to you, too. You know as much about this business as I do. You know about Grandfather's will, the ridiculous hoops the old man is making me jump through just to maintain control of this company, and you know what happens if I fail."

All she could do was nod. She'd been struck dumb and doubted she'd ever be able to speak again.

"Help me, Faith. Marry me. It's only for one year, and then we'll divorce. You're the ideal person to help me with this. You know how much McKay Corporation means to me, and you can do this without getting involved. With you and me, nothing will change."

Nothing will change. Reality struck her with a cold slap, effectively breaking the self-induced spell of Ryan's proposal. Of course. This proposal was just business. It wasn't a declaration of love. There was nothing personal in his motives.

Heat spread across her cheeks. How could she have thought someone like him could possibly have any feelings for her? One simple touch of his hand and she'd conjured up a full-blown fantasy of love and marriage. Her mother would have laughed if she could see her now. Laughed and told her how ridiculous she was.

What was she thinking? She was twenty-six years old, not sixteen. The time of girlish dreams was behind her, long ago replaced by a gritty reality that had nothing to do with romance and love.

"Faith?"

She raised her eyes to his. "Yes?"

Ryan squeezed her hands. "Are you all right?"

"I'm fine."

"If you're sure..."

"Yes, Mr. McKay, I'm sure." She maintained a level gaze with his and almost smiled at his look of concern. It probably wouldn't be good for his next intended bride to drop dead, considering he was rapidly running out of time and she was obviously his last choice.

"So, will you marry me?"

"Wh...what were the terms again?" She should know the terms. She'd quoted every line of the contract to Erica not more than a half hour ago, frantically trying to get Ryan's fiancée to change her mind about backing out of the wedding. But for some reason, her mind had just gone completely blank.

"I'll get the contract."

Her eyes followed his retreating form, the custom-made tux fitting his broad shoulders perfectly. Could she really do this? Could she marry Ryan McKay, become his wife, bear his child, and then a year later go back to the way things were before? How could she sleep with someone, share his life every day for a year and then act as if it hadn't happened?

But that's exactly what he expected of her. She tried her best to appear calm and professional when he returned with the papers.

"Here's the document. Read it carefully, because you have to be certain you can handle all the stipulations."

Faith nodded and, with shaky hands, took the contract from him. Trying to kick her brain into gear, she carefully read every word. It didn't take long to refresh her memory. After all, she'd read it over what seemed like a thousand times with Ryan, trying to find the loophole that would free him from Quentin McKay's marriage mandate.

"I can't believe your grandfather is forcing you to marry just to maintain control of McKay Corporation. It's so Middle Ages," she grumbled, suddenly feeling a personal stake in this.

Ryan cracked a smile and Faith sucked in a breath. Gone was the austere businessman, replaced instead by a charming, incredibly handsome man. Her heart picked up its frantic pace again.

He was a heartbreaker. He could literally break hers if she let emotions enter into this relationship. Admittedly, she was attracted to him, but what happened if she fell in love? Could her heart take a chance on caring for someone who didn't have the capacity to care back? And what about sex?

"What *about* sex?" he asked.

Had she said that last sentence out loud? Oh, no—she had! "Excuse me?"

"You asked me about sex. What do you want to know about it?"

Quickly she looked for an emergency of some sort that would untangle her foot from her errant mouth. Even a small trash fire would do. Nothing. "Um, I assume we'll be having it?"

He nodded, his wicked smile blowing away the darkness in his eyes, revealing the passion she'd always suspected lurked underneath. Only it had never been directed at her. Until now.

"Yes, Faith, we'll have to have sex to make a baby. Starting tonight."

A tingle began at her throat and moved steadily downward, touching every female part of her. For the first time in her life she was aware of herself as a woman and flushed with sudden heat. Her mind went into sexual overdrive, imagining the two of them twined together under satin sheets, sharing intimate whispers and caresses until...

Oh, no, this would never do. She couldn't possibly make love with him. She needed time. Time to steel her heart against falling in love. "That won't work for me."

He flashed her a devastating grin. "Kind of hard to fulfill the terms of the agreement without the sex part."

"I could be inseminated," she blurted, then cringed. She couldn't help but wrinkle her nose at the thought. So clinical. But, still—sex with Ryan McKay?

"No, we can't. Have you forgotten? Grandfather specified that conception could occur only by natural means, unless medically indicated."

"Right. I forgot. Anyway, I'm not ready for that to happen...tonight." Would she ever be ready?

"This isn't your typical situation, Faith. There are no rules about how long we have to be together. We're not going to date for several months and do things the traditional way."

"I know, but—"

"It's strictly business, with sex thrown in the mix. And sex is nothing more than biology, anyway."

The smoky heat of his gaze traveling over her body felt as tangible as if he'd actually touched her. She was grateful for the heavy suit of wool armor she wore, effectively masking the instant hardening of her nipples.

Her body had picked a fine time to come to sexual life. "I need some time, Ryan. I'm not accustomed to...to..."

"Not accustomed to having sex?" His eyes held a teasing gleam.

"That's not what I meant at all." How could she have let this subject come up?

"You *have* had sex before, haven't you?"

She shot back without thinking. "Of course I have. Lots of times!"

"Faith." He raised stern brows, daring her to lie. A pointless tactic on his part. She was never good at it anyway.

"Yes?" She contemplated her hands, clasped tightly together in her lap.

"Don't avoid the subject. Have you had sex before?"

She couldn't answer. It was too embarrassing.

"You're a virgin."

Could the day get any worse? How much more humiliation could she suffer? She nodded, mortified that he'd figured it out without her admission.

"Good God, Faith, why?"

"I was waiting."

"For what? The next millennium?"

For what, indeed. For a man, obviously. She'd never even had a serious boyfriend. She'd tried the dating thing a few times, but failed miserably.

And now, hearing it from Ryan, she felt more than a little ridiculous. A twenty-six-year-old virgin. About to marry a man who had probably bedded more women than she cared to know about.

"I was waiting for love. For the right man. I don't know. I was just waiting." She stood and walked to the window, the lights of Las Vegas mocking her. They were towering glitz and

19

glamour, offering up every delicious sin available to anyone who wanted it. She was short, plain and undesirable, with absolutely nothing of value to offer.

He stepped behind her, his breath blowing against her neck. "Don't be embarrassed. It's endearing. Refreshing, actually."

"It's pathetic." She felt miserable, not endearing. Something so personal, so intimate, and of all the people in the world to find out about it, it had to be Ryan.

He touched her shoulders lightly, and sparks flew. A shock, a tingle and then heat.

"It's not pathetic. Turn around and look at me."

She couldn't. He forced her by gently turning her shoulders. She lifted her lashes, expecting to see the ridicule in his eyes, but found only compassion. And interest.

"I think you need to consider this proposal more seriously." He looked at his watch for the millionth time in the past hour. "I don't want you to do something you'll regret."

He was giving her an out. She could decline the offer and still keep her job.

But in five years she'd never let Ryan McKay down. And she wasn't going to let a silly thing like her virginity stand in the way. Besides, wasn't it about time she had a life? Granted, this wasn't quite what she had in mind, but it beat sitting in her apartment reading books every night.

So he didn't love her. So what? Did she have a better offer sitting on the table at the moment? Any prospects? Hardly. And this was her chance to gain a little experience—check that— knowing what she knew about Ryan, a lot of experience, in the sex department. She had nothing to lose, and everything to gain. As long as she remembered that this was a business deal only. As long as she remembered to guard her heart.

"There's nothing further to consider, Mr. McKay. As you stated, this is strictly business. Let's go back to the contract, shall we?"

"Are you sure?"

She nodded quickly before she changed her mind. At Ryan's suggestion, they moved to the table in the center of the expansive living area and spread the contract over the large glass top.

She recited the terms she already knew all too well. They sounded completely different when she related them to herself. "We have to stay married for one year, and during that time we must sleep together in the same bedroom." She forced herself to block out the images of his hands, his mouth, his body.

"Correct."

"And I have to become pregnant within that year."

"Right. If no pregnancy occurs, we have to spend another year together and undergo fertility testing until you conceive. And if you can't by then, we divorce, you get a settlement, and this whole search-for-a-bride circus starts all over again for me."

He'd stated the terms so impersonally, yet Faith knew how much this whole charade bothered him. More than once over the past year he'd ranted to her about his manipulating grandfather. If he'd wanted a wife, he'd told her, he'd have damn well gone out and found one himself.

"I'm just going to have to hope you can bear children," he added.

Faith shrugged. "Obviously, I have no idea. And you have to be able to...um ..."

"Provide the fertilizer?" He offered a wry smile. "I'd already looked into that as a possible loophole. If I were sterile, this

21

entire deal would be off. Unfortunately, or fortunately, depending on how you look at it, I have plenty of strong swimmers in me."

Faith chose to ignore the implications of that statement and focused instead on the contract. "Who will monitor our marriage?"

Ryan's eyes darkened with his frown. "My cousin, James, who stands to inherit the business if I fail, as well as Grandfather's attorney, Stan Fredericks. They'll be shadowing us like a couple of PIs in a bad Bogart movie. Watching our every move, making sure we sleep in the same room, insuring we're always together."

Wonderful. It would be like living with a camera in her face for the next year. "And if you travel, I have to go with you."

"That's right. As will James and Stan. And don't forget, we have to appear before the board every month to report on the state of our marriage."

"Yes, I remember that part." She handed the paper back to him. "And the child we create. You want no part of it."

He nodded. "I don't want a child, nor do I need a family. This whole ordeal is because my grandfather had some misguided notion while on his deathbed that he needed to redeem himself. And so he thought he could show me the love he never had by forcing me into a marriage I don't want, and require me to have a child I have no intention of raising."

Ryan shrugged and turned to the window. He was so tired of playing this ridiculous game. And now he'd had to draw Faith into it.

She was the only one who understood and accepted him. Who had no expectations of him. Unlike his grandfather.

As if Quentin McKay had even known what love was. His grandfather had never shown even a glimpse of it to the frightened eight-year-old boy whose father had died and whose mother decided she'd rather play socialite than parent.

He'd witnessed the loveless marriage of both his parents and his grandparents, and never wanted to personally experience it himself. Now his grandfather was forcing him to do the same thing—marry for anything but love. This was Quentin McKay's way of making amends?

"I'm sorry." Faith's soft voice brought him back to reality. He turned toward her and offered a smile. She'd always made him feel better.

Marriage to Faith for a year would be easy. Despite the dowdy outfits and huge glasses she wore, and the way she tried to hide her sable hair in those horrid buns, she was attractive.

Not beautiful like Erica, but then again Erica was so remote she was practically untouchable. If she hadn't been so hungry for the settlement money she'd have never entertained the notion of marrying him. It wasn't like she'd agreed to the marriage out of any caring or love for him.

But Faith? She would do it because she was loyal to him. Dedicated, and with a shy quality that Ryan found foreign in his usual social circle. She oozed desirability in a way that had nothing to do with expensive clothes, artfully applied makeup or pedigree.

Faith was genuine, honest and caring. And a natural beauty. The thought of making love to her ran through his mind. And not simply for the act of procreation. He could already imagine unlocking the secrets she tried so hard to hide away.

He'd caught glimpses of them. The way she looked at him when she thought he wasn't looking. The way her eyes lit up when he entered a room. Her willingness to do anything to help

Jaci Burton

him with the business. The way her voice softened when she
spoke to him.

"Are you certain you're willing to sign away rights to our
child?"

The harsh reality of her question shook him out of his
fantasies of making love to her. What would he do with a child?
Treat it the way he'd been treated? He'd never put a child
through what he'd been through. What had he been thinking
asking Erica to marry him? What kind of mother would she
have made? The same kind of father he'd make, no doubt. That
was the problem with this deal. He hadn't been thinking
straight—not since he'd been read the terms of his
grandfather's will.

Ryan had already accepted the fact that he didn't have the
capacity to love. He'd had no loving role models. No, he wasn't
cut out to be a father. He felt a twinge, something unfamiliar as
he looked at Faith and imagined that pixie smile on a tiny boy.
His boy. Theirs.

Quickly and coldly he banished the image from his mind
and addressed Faith's question. She, at least, would be a good
mother to the child they created. That eased his conscience
somewhat.

"I'll sign away rights and you'll get a handsome settlement,
full support and expenses for the rest of the child's life. You'll
be well taken care of financially, Faith. You and your child."

Faith studied him, his voice so cold and detached. He
couldn't even refer to the baby they'd make as *their* child or *his*
child. Even in this, she'd be alone. Like she'd always been.
Unwanted, unloved. With a child whose father didn't love or
want it. Could she do that?

Then again, this child would have a mother who did love
and want it. That's where things would be different. She'd give

her child all the love she'd never received from her own mother. And twice that amount to equal its missing father.

"There's also the money," he continued. "Don't forget about the five million dollar settlement you'll receive when the marriage ends. You and your child will never want for anything."

"Money isn't relevant. I have everything I need right now." The things she'd craved, had always desired, had very little to do with money.

So why was she contemplating doing this? To help Ryan, of course. She'd do anything for him, and always had. That was her job, wasn't it?

Face it. Her job was her life. She *was* pathetic.

"It all sounds fine, Mr. McKay."

"I think it's time you called me Ryan."

"All right. Ryan." How strange, after all these years, to call him by his first name.

"Then it's settled."

"Umm, there's just one more thing."

He waited.

The sex thing still nagged at her. She was hesitant to broach the subject, but the mere thought of it caused nausea to rise up in her throat. She had to bring it up. "Before we continue, we need to discuss the sex part."

"What about the sex part?"

How was she going to approach this? She'd never asked Ryan McKay for anything the entire time she'd worked for him. And now she was going to mess with his intentions for this agreement.

"Sex is something I don't take lightly. It means something to me. A sharing of feelings, of deep emotion."

His eyes narrowed and turned an icy gray. "I don't have feelings, Faith. For you or anyone else. Don't mistake any physical desire I may show as emotion or caring. You'll only end up hurting yourself."

She'd already surmised that, even though his nearness unnerved her, awakened yearnings she'd never had before. He was right about biology and sex. She could already picture them naked together, their bodies entwined in a ritual older than both of them. But not tonight.

"I know. But still, I'd like a little time. It may be purely physical and unemotional for you, Ryan, but sex will never be that way for me. I'm sorry, but I'm just not ready."

Ryan looked at his watch, his face drawn into a hard line. Guilt punched her in the gut. She'd disappointed him. But what could she do?

"What kind of time frame are you talking about?" he asked.

How about forever? Okay, that wasn't realistic. But she'd take as much as he would give. She needed time to figure out how she could allow him to make love to her without leaving feelings behind when it was over. "Three months."

"I had hoped to have you pregnant in three months."

She'd always been impressed by his confidence. "I'm sorry, but I just can't do it right away. Everything else in the agreement looks fine. But I have to have three months."

"I'll give you two."

Two months. At least it would buy her some time to adjust. "Fine. Two months."

"Do we have an agreement?"

Not quite the proposal of marriage Faith had always dreamed of, but then again her life hadn't turned out like she'd imagined either. "Yes, I'll marry you."

"Great. I'll get Stan up here right away with a new contract."

Cell phone against his ear, he'd already dismissed her. Not surprising. She knew what she was getting into when she agreed to this, so she shouldn't be disappointed at the lack of romance in his proposal. This was the way their marriage would be, and she'd made the bargain with her eyes wide open.

After all, to Ryan it was nothing personal. But to Faith, it was much more. She had just agreed to sign over her life, and if she wasn't careful, her heart, to Ryan McKay.

Chapter Two

Faith pored over the wedding dresses the ladies from the boutique had brought over. The last hour had been a whirlwind of activities, from signing the contract to selecting a dress. She wanted to pinch herself to be certain this wasn't all a dream— some fantasy she'd concocted in her mind about the wedding she'd always wanted but never thought she'd have.

She glanced at Ryan. He seemed perfectly at ease, leaning against the bar and sipping a drink. "How did they know what sizes to bring?" she asked.

He shrugged, clearly uninterested in the dress selection. "I looked at you and made a guess."

Good guess. But how had he known? She thought he never looked at her. She felt his eyes on her now, watching as she chose a dress.

The sequin and pearl tulle gown she selected had a satin bodice and dropped shoulders. The waist was snug and led to a bell skirt that looked like something Cinderella would wear. The veil had a tiara with the same pearls and sequins as the dress.

As a child she'd dreamed of her wedding day—what little girl hadn't? Never in her wildest imaginings would it have been anything this grand. She was the princess on her way to the ball. There was even a handsome prince waiting for her.

The ladies of the boutique laid out a selection of shoes, stockings and undergarments. Faith selected a pair of satin pumps and some decadent silk underthings. Not like she had much choice. Didn't these people make anything out of cotton?

Ryan approached her. "I've made arrangements for the court clerk to issue our marriage license immediately. You've got about a half hour to get ready. I'll be back to get you." He placed his empty glass on the bar and headed toward the door.

She nodded and he left. So much for acting the part of the prince. It was time to get a grip. This was business, not a fairy tale. And she had a half hour to turn from dowdy secretary to blushing bride. It was a good thing her hair was already up and she didn't wear makeup.

Elma and Vivian from the bridal shop offered to stay and help her dress. She was grateful, because her hands shook so badly she couldn't have buttoned a thing. The tiny pearl buttons from the scoop back all the way down below her rear end were impossible for her to reach. She'd have never gotten into it by herself.

As she slipped on the strapless satin bra, Faith was embarrassed that Ryan had guessed at her small cup size. She released a wistful sigh at her minimal dimensions and silently thanked Ryan for helping her avoid the mortification of having to stuff socks in some dress that was too big. She'd stopped doing that when she was twelve after her mother found out and chastised her for trying to be something she wasn't.

After the women left, Faith took a couple minutes to stare at her reflection in the suite's mirrored closet doors. She couldn't believe the transformation. The dress fit as if it had been sewed on her. The skirt was full, with seed pearls and rhinestones sprinkled throughout the tulle netting like fairy dust. The bodice was tight and with the bra she'd chosen at least pushed her tiny breasts up enough to generate a modicum of cleavage. It was low cut, but not enough that she'd need a stapler to hold it to her chest.

The women had insisted on a little makeup despite Faith's objections. Admittedly, they'd been right. At least she now had some color in her cheeks. Before, she'd looked less like a bride and more like a prisoner about to be led to the gallows.

"Okay, Faith," she said to her reflection. "This is the best you can do with what God gave you. I hope you don't disappoint your husband-to-be."

"Believe me. I'm not disappointed."

She whirled at the sound of Ryan's voice. "I didn't see you there," she said, feeling like she'd been caught playing dress up in someone else's clothes.

Her heart raced at the sight of him, so elegantly perfect in his well-tailored tux that she forgot to breathe. The crisp white shirt made a sharp contrast against his tanned face and neck.

His eyes never left hers as he lifted her hand. A rush of anxiety fluttered deep within her that had little to do with stressful business arrangements or marriages of convenience.

"You look beautiful." His voice vibrated through her nerve endings and she went from heated to shivering in an instant.

But he was just being polite. Clothes couldn't change her looks, but she appreciated the attempt. "Thank you," she replied. "So do you."

He laughed then, deep and masculine, and her body tingled in response.

"But something's missing from your wardrobe."

"It is?" Faith looked down. She had the dress, shoes, underwear. Everything seemed perfectly in place.

"Yes. This." Ryan drew a black velvet box out of his breast pocket.

Faith looked up at him, uncertain what to do. He opened the box to reveal a diamond choker that had to be worth a fortune. Surely he didn't mean those for her.

"Are these on loan from Lucy's?"

"No, they're my wedding gift to you. Turn around."

A wedding gift. She hadn't expected it, and couldn't stop her heart from soaring. Could this fairy tale be real?

Faith turned to face the mirror, watching as Ryan took the necklace out of the box and held the clasps in each hand. He reached around her and laid the necklace against her collarbone, lightly brushing the tiny swell of her breasts with the sides of his hands. As he pulled the necklace up and fastened it, she took a quick breath and shivered.

Instead of removing his hands after the necklace was fastened, Ryan rested them lightly on the tops of her shoulders, pressing his fingers into her flesh. Faith was certain he could hear her heart pounding, its rapid thrums echoing in her ears like thunder.

"There." He stepped away to examine her. "That's better."

Her hand crept to the diamonds sparkling at her throat. This couldn't be happening to her. It was someone else standing in front of the mirror, looking like a princess in a gorgeous wedding gown and glittering diamonds. If she didn't know better, she would think it was her real wedding day and she was a woman with the blush of love tingeing her cheeks. But she *did* know better.

"Thank you," she said to Ryan as she turned away from the mirror to face him. "The necklace is lovely, the dress is beautiful and I feel like Cinderella."

The trace of a smile on his generous lips disappeared. He stepped away from her. "It's not a fairy tale, Faith. This is business. Don't put your heart in it or you'll end up getting hurt."

Too late. She hurt already from the bite of his words. But they were also true. This wasn't her fairy tale wedding, and Ryan McKay certainly wasn't her Prince Charming.

"I'll be right outside the suite. Come out when you're ready," he said and then exited the room.

Just business. That's all it would ever be. They weren't two people in love making the commitment of their lives today. They were coworkers about to close a business deal.

She couldn't help but want it to be more. This was, after all, her first wedding. And even if it was a farce, she was going to enjoy it as if it were real.

They took the elevator downstairs. Whispers and well wishes were directed their way as they wound around the intricate maze through the casino and towards the lobby. Faith smiled shyly at all the people who stopped to offer congratulations. She'd never been noticed before, and to have this kind of attention was overwhelming. It had to be the dress and sparkling diamonds at her throat. Even the dullest mannequin would be noticed when a designer dress and jewels worth a fortune were draped over it.

The lobby bustled with activity. It was Friday night and the weekend gamblers filled the hotel and casino. Faith loved this hotel, with its alabaster figurines and golden draperies perfectly complementing the stunning gold and white marble floor. For the first time she felt like she belonged here. She sailed across the lobby, the heels of her white satin shoes tapping in time to the frantic beat of her heart.

Ryan stopped at the concierge's desk and whispered to the young gentleman on duty. The man nodded at Ryan's orders and wished them both luck.

They entered a second set of elevators that would take them to the chapel. What was Ryan thinking about all this? This moment was so special to her, and she wanted to remember this evening as if it were in actuality the wedding of her dreams. It was quite possibly the only wedding she'd ever have. But what about him? Did he dread the moment when he would be bound to her for the next year?

The elevator opened into a lobby of dark, polished wood and solid brass. Huge double doors greeted them with the words *Chalet Wedding Chapel* emblazoned in gold letters across the top of the archway. Ryan led her through the doors, the last time she'd enter a room as a single woman. For the next year, anyway.

A petite woman with short dark hair rushed over to them. Miriam Snelling was the Chalet Chapel's efficient and nononsense wedding coordinator.

"Mr. McKay," she gushed with enthusiasm as she shook Ryan's hand, "I'm so pleased you decided to have your wedding with us." The woman's eyebrows arched in surprise when she saw Faith, but other than a polite greeting, the woman didn't voice whatever opinion she harbored about Ryan's choice of a bride.

Faith knew what the woman thought.

"Thank you, Miss Snelling," he replied. "We're running short of time. Is everything ready?"

"Yes, of course." Miss Snelling ushered them into a waiting room. "The minister will be in shortly to fill out the forms and then we can get started."

They waited in awkward silence for the minister. Faith threaded her fingers together, her gaze traveling to her left hand.

No rings.

"Ryan, we don't have wedding rings."

"It's all taken care of," he replied. "Don't worry."

She should have known he'd see to every detail. A gentleman arrived carrying a brown leather case. Faith recognized him as Bradley Peters, the manager of Lucy's Diamonds, an upscale jewelry store at the hotel. Ryan instructed him to put the case on the minister's desk and beckoned Faith to come over.

"Mr. McKay would like you to select rings," Bradley said as he opened the case to reveal dozens of diamond wedding rings.

Faith looked at Ryan.

"Go ahead, pick something out that you like. But be quick about it," he said.

She peered into the case and examined the men's rings. It didn't take her long to find one she liked, a simple yellow and white gold band with love knots woven throughout and two small diamonds nestled inside the loops of an infinity circle.

"I like this one," she said as she held it up for Ryan's inspection. "Do you?"

He shrugged. "Whichever one you like is fine with me."

"Please, at least look at it. Try it on to make sure it fits." His approval of her selection meant something, even if the exchange of rings to signify a forever bond was as fake as his feelings for her.

Ryan sighed and took the ring from her fingers. It fit him perfectly and looked just like Faith imagined it would. Masculine, yet not too frail or garish.

"It's very nice," he said as he took the ring off and handed it back to the jeweler. "Now, pick one for yourself."

"For me? I couldn't possibly. You do it."

He glared at her, but she resisted. She absolutely wasn't going to be able to choose her own ring. Finally, he bent over the jewelry case. Faith was surprised he didn't choose the first ring his hand grasped, considering they had about a half hour left before the deadline, coupled with his complete lack of interest. But he examined all of them, then took her hand in his to examine her fingers. After perusing several, he selected one.

"Do you like this one?"

What wasn't there to like? She was astounded that he had picked the same one that had caught her eye. The gold band matched the ring she'd selected for him, except the love knots encircled a huge marquise-shaped diamond that had to be over two carats. Faith would have never selected a ring like that for herself, even if it was the most beautiful one in the case.

"It's breathtaking. Of course, I like it. But isn't it a bit expensive?"

Mr. Peters stifled a cough and Ryan just smiled. "We'll take these two, Bradley."

"Yes, sir." The jeweler produced two black boxes, slipped their rings inside and handed them to Ryan. Then he quickly made his exit as the minister entered.

"Hello, Ryan," Reverend Dodd said in a friendly voice as he turned to Faith. "And you must be...oh. Miss Lewis."

Obviously, the minister expected Erica, and was quite surprised to find Faith standing there.

"Reverend, there's been a slight change in brides." Ryan's tone brooked no further conversation.

"Well. I can see that," he said with a smile.

Right, Faith thought. Erica, the big star, couldn't make the performance so Faith, the understudy, had stepped in.

They finished the paperwork in minutes, Faith barely able to give her full name to Reverend Dodd, let alone remember her date of birth. She only heard bits and pieces of the minister's spiel on how the ceremony would proceed, her thoughts focusing primarily on this decision and what she'd just gotten herself into.

After Reverend Dodd left with Ryan, Miriam appeared.

"Well, dear," Miriam said upon her return. "May I say you are absolutely stunning this evening. You make a gorgeous bride and I'm sure you and Mr. McKay will be very happy together."

Faith tried a smile, but her lips quivered as reality hit her. She was getting married. Not to the man she'd desired for so long, but to the man who was her boss.

Miriam handed her a bouquet of white roses. With shaky hands Faith lifted them to her nose. Their sweet fragrance brought tears to her eyes for so many different reasons. She wished this was a marriage based on love and lifetime commitment instead of the contract she had signed. Someday, maybe her fairy tale dreams would come true.

The chapel was decorated in soft white and pastel blue. White lilies attached to trailing blue satin ribbons adorned each row. Faith couldn't have picked a more beautiful place for her wedding.

She hoped she wouldn't collapse in a dead faint, throw up or turn tail and run screaming from the room. Instead, she held a death grip on the quivering rose bouquet, managed a tremulous smile and headed down the aisle toward her intended husband.

The minister smiled indulgently, Ryan looked impatient and Faith was trying to remember how to breathe. Flashbulbs blinded her progress as the photographer followed her every move, snapping shots by the second. She hated being photographed, but she knew from having made the arrangements that this entire shebang, from the dress and Ryan's tux to the chapel and photographs, was all about PR. It would be good for the company, and that's what mattered. She tried to smile and not look sick.

It was the longest walk of her life. When she finally reached the altar, Ryan took her shaking hand and placed it in the crook of his left arm.

This was it.

The minister spoke about love, honor, commitment and everlasting fidelity. She tried to focus on the words and their meaning, but she was distracted by Ryan's warm hand covering hers, his thumb tracing lazy circles over the top of her hand. His nearness unnerved her and all he was doing was standing next to her. How was she going to handle living with him? Sleeping with him?

She forced her mind back to the here and now. Reverend Dodd said a few words about the sanctity of their marriage, and then...

"By the power vested in me by the State of Nevada, I now pronounce you husband and wife. Mr. McKay, you may kiss your bride."

That was it? They were married?

Ryan turned to Faith and she forced herself to meet his gaze. He graced her with a generous smile and leaned towards her.

She was supposed to kiss him. The man she'd worked side by side with for the past five years and had barely shaken hands with, and she was supposed to kiss him. Her boss. Her drop-dead gorgeous, sexy, virile boss. Who also happened to now be her husband. Surely he'd give her a quick peck on the lips and that would be all.

She was wrong.

He slid his arms around her and drew her against his chest, effectively cutting off what remaining oxygen fueled her numb brain. His gray eyes darkened at the same time he pressed his lips against hers.

Her breath caught on a sigh as his soft lips caressed her trembling mouth before capturing it in a firm kiss that shocked Faith to her toes. Lightning struck her heart, electricity arcing through her as his tongue entered her mouth and boldly twined with hers.

It was a promise of delicious things to come. Things Faith wanted right this moment, yet also feared more than nightmares in the dark.

This had to be the most passionate kiss Faith had ever received.

As soon as it began, it was over. Yet that brief kiss had seemed to last an eternity. Ryan released her and stepped back, appearing unaffected by their kiss as he turned away.

It was as if they had kissed a thousand times instead of this being their first. Faith, on the other hand, stood like a statue, completely stunned by the entire ceremony and the resulting kiss.

"Are you all right?" Ryan asked.

Her lips still burned, but she managed a nod. "Yes, I'm fine. This is all kind of overwhelming."

"It's been an eventful day for you."

"That's an understatement."

"Well, it's over now. Let's go."

Faith stopped him. "Where are we going?"

"To my house."

"What about the things at my apartment?"

"I've already made arrangements for them to be packed up and moved to the house. You'll have them by morning."

"But, I have nothing to wear other than the clothes I worked in today and this dress. I don't have a toothbrush, comb, shampoo—"

"Relax, Faith," he interrupted as he grabbed her hand and headed toward the door. "I've already anticipated the things you'll need and they'll be at the house when we arrive."

Ryan's attorney stood outside the chapel, smiling brightly.

"Looks like you made the deadline, Ryan. Barely."

"Yes, it's done, Stan, and the terms of the will are met."

Stan nodded. "So far so good. But there's still more to come in order to complete the mandates."

"I'm fully aware of that," Ryan said crisply. "Now if you don't mind, it's been a long damn day and I'd like to get out of here."

"Of course," Stan said and turned to Faith. "Congratulations, Mrs. McKay, and I wish you the best of luck in your marriage." He quickly made his exit from the room.

Mrs. McKay. Reality struck home. She was married. To Ryan McKay. And now she was going home with him to begin a year filled with uncertainty.

Why had she done this? To help her boss? Or because deep down she had yearned for this, hoped someone, someday would ask her to marry him?

It didn't matter now. The deed was done. She hoped she'd made the right decision, because her entire life had just changed dramatically.

Chapter Three

No doubt about it, Faith had transformed from a working girl into a princess right before his eyes. Ryan watched the sway of her full skirt as she headed down the hallway towards the elevators. She walked with a natural, sexy little swish of her hips and that dress accentuated it.

What was he doing? Already salivating behind his new wife and they hadn't even been married an hour. He forced his eyes away from her backside and thought about the upcoming business deal he'd had to put off because of this ridiculous wedding charade. That's what he needed to concentrate on. Business was his only driving desire. Not some attractive brunette's rear end.

But it was such a nice rear end. Even covered in all that white and lacy wedding dress stuff. Or when she hid it under long granny skirts and suit jackets too big for her petite frame. Ryan had a keen eye and a very vivid imagination. An imagination that already had Faith undressed and waiting for him on his bed.

If he were honest with himself, he'd admit she had knocked him off his feet when he walked into the bedroom of the penthouse to find her standing there in her wedding gown. He'd never bothered to ask her why she hid her beauty under thick glasses that didn't fit her face, or kept her hair severely pulled back into an ugly roll.

He would never ask. That would be personal, and Ryan never got personal.

But despite her best efforts at camouflage, she was incapable of hiding her natural beauty. And the wedding dress had somehow transformed her. Her eyes shined like a sunlit ocean and her cheeks glowed with a natural blush that had nothing to do with makeup. She even looked happy. A ridiculous notion since theirs was nothing but a business marriage.

When he'd caught her reflection in the mirror at the suite, Ryan had felt like he was the man she was destined to be with. The one whose touch would flame her desire. Like she had flamed his. He felt like today was his real wedding day and Faith was his real wife. And tonight was his wedding night.

The tightening in his tux trousers annoyed him more than his errant thoughts. He never had more than a fleeting interest in a woman. To give more than random attention meant emotional involvement, and he'd learned well from his parents and grandfather that emotion led to hurt.

Where would he ever have learned to care for someone? His mother was a socialite with no use for a child, his father a workaholic who'd driven himself into an early grave, and his grandfather lacked even a rudimentary knowledge of warmth and love. He'd had no role models, so where would he have learned how to give his heart?

Women were for physical release or to grace his arm at a social or business function. And that was it. Females like that were available in ample abundance in Las Vegas. They never occupied his thoughts for longer than the time necessary to deal with them. Then they were gone. They got what they wanted out of the relationship, and so did he, and no one got hurt.

Except Faith was different. She wasn't going to go away. And apparently wasn't going to leave his thoughts either, despite his efforts to direct his mind to business instead of imagining what she wore under her wedding dress.

Why now? She'd been with him for five years, day in and day out. He'd hired her because she came recommended right out of college, graduating at the top of her class from the University of Las Vegas. She was sharp, unassuming and didn't show interest in him at all. In fact, she avoided even incidental personal contact like the plague.

Just what he needed in an executive assistant. Business only.

But underneath her capable exterior was an innocence he'd been unaware of. And that intrigued him.

Why was Faith still a virgin? And why did the thought of sex terrify her?

That, he definitely wanted to change.

They stopped at the elevator and Faith turned to him, her blue eyes staring expectantly.

"Are we going to your home now?" she asked in that soft voice that poured over him like a well-aged brandy.

"Yes."

She swallowed and turned away to wait for the elevator. Without further discussion on the ride down in the elevator, they headed through the hotel and outside into the cool April air.

Faith inhaled deeply, savoring the crisp oxygen and willed her hands to stop shaking. Involuntary shivers began as soon as they'd walked outside. The wind had kicked up and her sleeveless dress did nothing to avert the chill.

"Cold?" Ryan asked.

"A little."

"Here. Put this on." He removed his tux jacket and draped it over her shoulders. Faith felt his body heat radiating from the silk lining and instinctively pulled the jacket tighter around her to get closer to his warmth. It carried his scent, a combination of musky cologne and something purely Ryan.

The sleek black limousine pulled up and Ryan helped her inside.

"These things always remind me of hotel rooms, minus the bed," Faith said as she settled in and surveyed the expansive interior of the limo.

She'd been in plenty of them before, but always as Ryan's assistant. She'd never paid much attention to what they looked like. Would she be riding in them more often now?

The seats were soft, cushiony leather that she sank into. Her voluminous gown billowed around her until she was surrounded by tulle. It was a full service limo, with a television, wet bar and telephone within reach.

"It has its luxuries," Ryan replied dryly.

"Why didn't we take your car?"

"I thought you'd be more comfortable riding in the limo, considering your dress, rather than trying to stuff you into the BMW."

"Oh. That makes sense." He'd put her comfort first. He'd actually thought about her. Amazing. Just like the entire evening—simply unbelievable.

Faith focused outside the tinted windows, watching as passenger cars pulled alongside. She smiled as people in the other cars squinted as if trying to guess what celebrity lurked inside. She'd done the same thing before, wondering what life was like on the other side of the mirrored glass. Funny, she still felt like one of those people on the outside.

"Would you like some music?"

She nodded and Ryan hit one of the many buttons located on the door console of the limo. Soft classical poured from the speakers. She took a deep breath and forced herself to relax by closing her eyes and listening to the lulling sounds. She tried not to think about where she was going, or what kind of life she was heading into for the next year.

They traveled well outside the city limits and into the residential areas of the county. The limo slowed at the gated community where the McKay mansion was located. It was very high security, complete with electronic surveillance cameras and a fierce-looking guard at the entrance.

Ryan rolled down the back window, and the guard approached. He smiled when he saw Ryan.

"Evening, Mr. McKay," the guard said. "Go right on through."

"Thanks, Tom," Ryan said and rolled the window back up.

Once through the gate, Faith peered through the darkened windows to better see the enormous homes they passed as they wound their way through the streets of the community. It was dark, but the houses were all well lit. She'd been this way several times, but had never paid attention to her surroundings. Back then, this neighborhood didn't signify her home. Now it did.

The limo stopped in front of a familiar imposing structure— the McKay mansion. Like something out of a movie, the brick facade and towers made it look more a castle than a house.

Ryan exited the vehicle and held out his hand for Faith, which she gratefully grasped for assistance out of the limo. It wasn't easy maneuvering in this big, poofy dress.

The heavy wood door loomed before her. She tried to swallow but her throat had gone dry.

When they approached the door it opened automatically. He directed her inside and Leland Banks, Ryan's butler, greeted them.

"Good evening, Mr. McKay," the man said formally in his very proper British accent.

"Evening, Leland," Ryan answered.

"And a very good evening to you, Mrs. McKay. May I offer my congratulations to you both?"

Ryan must have notified Leland of their marriage. Whatever thoughts the butler had about it were masked completely by his stoic demeanor.

"Thanks, Leland. Could you show Mrs. McKay to the second bedroom? It's late and I still have some things to catch up on."

"But I thought the contract said..." Faith clamped her lips shut and looked to Ryan, not knowing how much he had revealed to Leland about the terms of the will.

"I know the contract states we sleep in the same bedroom," Ryan explained, "but Stan and James won't arrive until tomorrow and I don't want to keep you up all night. I have work to do."

Which meant he really didn't want her in his bedroom. Faith pushed aside the feeling of being dumped. After all, this two-month waiting period had been her idea. But still, they would have to sleep together, so why not tonight?

She was being silly. Instead of feeling rejected, she should be glad for the one-night reprieve.

Ryan disappeared down the hall and Leland led Faith to the staircase beyond the huge marble foyer. "If you'll come this way, ma'am."

Faith had been in the house a few times to assist Ryan with business functions, but had never been in more than a couple of the rooms downstairs.

They took the spiral staircase to the second floor. Leland led her down the right side of the hallway toward a set of double doors. He opened them for her and stood aside, beckoning Faith to enter the room.

When she did, her mouth dropped open in shock. This wasn't a bedroom, it was a house. The thick Berber carpet felt like pillows under her feet. In the center of the room was a king-sized bed covered in a duvet of soft cream and roses with a matching canopy. It looked like a harem paradise, with pale cream and rose carpet and a very light, intricately arched headboard.

"Would you like something to eat, Mrs. McKay?"

Faith had all but forgotten Leland was in the room. "No, that's okay. It's late. I'll just wait until morning."

"Nonsense," Leland said. "Have you eaten tonight?"

Now that she thought of it, Faith hadn't had a thing to eat since lunch. "Not really."

"I'll bring something right up then."

While she waited, she explored the room. The bath was separated from the bedroom by white double doors. Faith walked through the doors and gasped as she stepped into a closet larger than her entire apartment.

She could have fit her living room furniture in there. And it was completely empty, except for a breathtakingly beautiful satin nightgown.

No other clothes. Big problem.

Leland's knock at the door brought her attention from the closet to her stomach. The tray he carried was filled with more food than Faith could eat in a day, let alone one sitting.

"Thank you so much for this, Leland." Faith's mouth watered at the feast Leland set on the table.

"You're welcome, Mrs. McKay."

"Please," she said, offering a small smile. "Call me Faith."

Leland shook his head. "It wouldn't be appropriate."

Faith frowned at him. "Why not?"

"Because it's not done. You are the mistress of this house, and I am a servant."

"Well, that's silly."

"It's the way things have always been done. We all have our station in life."

Did the man ever smile? Faith sat on the edge of her bed and studied the McKays' butler. "That's so middle ages. This is the twenty-first century, Leland. I think the lines between the social classes have smudged more than a little. Besides, it's not like you don't know me. I'm no different now than I was before."

Leland clasped his hands behind his back, his frame rigid and unyielding. "Oh, but you are, ma'am. Perhaps in your circles the masters and servants mix, but not in mine. I have been butler to the McKays for more than thirty-five years, and it has always been this way."

Faith drew her shoulders back and blew a frustrated sigh. She could tell she'd get nowhere with Leland tonight, and was too tired to debate.

"Enjoy your dinner, ma'am," he said as he inclined his head toward her and left the room.

The food made her stomach grumble, but first things first. A change of clothes. She did not want to attempt a meal with tulle stuffed up under her chin.

The moment she stepped into the dressing room it hit her. There was no way she could get out of her wedding dress without help. It was after one in the morning, and she had no idea where Leland had gone, or for that matter, her new husband. So who could assist her?

Maybe if she opened the door and yelled for help someone would come running. Faith pondered that option as she stepped out.

The hall was long and led to another set of double doors at the end. Was that Ryan's room?

She maneuvered the dark hallway until she reached the door at the opposite end from her own. She placed her ear against the door, listening for any sounds. Nothing. Well, whoever was in there was about to be awakened because she wasn't going to eat or sleep in her wedding dress.

Three swift knocks and she stepped back to wait. No answer. Maybe the room was empty and she was wasting her time. She knocked again, this time louder, and the door flung open, light shining on her from the brightly lit bedroom.

Ryan was still in his tux pants, but he'd removed the jacket and tie and almost completely unbuttoned the shirt.

Faith tried to find her voice, but the sight of her bare-chested husband took her breath away. He had an impressive build and a firm, muscular chest with a sprinkling of dark, curling hair.

He leaned against the doorway waiting for her to speak. "Did you want something?" he asked.

"I...I need some help." Now she stammered like a teenager. Wonderful impression she was making on her new husband.

"What kind of help?"

He didn't even invite her in. She felt like a salesperson attempting to sell a vacuum cleaner, fully expecting to have the door slammed in her face at any moment.

"I can't unbutton my dress."

Was she speaking another language? Why was he frowning?

"What do you mean?" he asked.

"I mean this," she said with more than a little frustration. She was tired, hungry and wanted to get out of the dress now more than anything in the world. "Look," she said and turned around for him to see her dilemma.

"I see. Okay, let's go."

"Go? Go where?" By the time she had the words out Ryan was heading towards her room. She lifted her skirt and hurried after him.

He entered her bedroom and waited for her to catch up. "Turn around," he commanded.

Faith did as she was told, more than a little embarrassed to have her new husband undressing her, despite the fact it was exactly what should happen on her wedding night. On a normal wedding night, maybe, but not this one.

She tried to stand patiently while Ryan slowly slipped each satin covered pearl button from its tiny loophole. But his touch did things to her sense of equilibrium. She shivered each time his warm knuckles brushed the bare skin of her back.

"Are you cold?" Ryan's voice whispered softly against her ear.

"Not really."

"You're shivering."

"Um...yes."

"Why?"

"I don't know." *Liar.*

Ryan's hands stilled. "Does my touch bother you?"

His touch most definitely bothered her. But not in the way he thought.

"No, it's fine. Go ahead."

She steeled herself against any more outward signs of his effect on her. It wouldn't do at all to fall into bed with him, no matter how much his skin on hers made her tingle. She'd made a bargain for two months and needed that time to get to know her new husband.

These were new sensations, new feelings, and her senses were already on overload from the day's events. She couldn't handle much more without a complete meltdown.

But then his hands moved lower as he freed the buttons near her bottom. The chills returned.

"I think there's enough undone now that I can get out of this thing," she stammered.

"Just a few more," he said, ignoring her request. Obviously his touch on her skin didn't affect him at all. "Do you need me to help you take it off?"

"No!" Faith cringed, not meaning for her denial to sound so forceful. She turned to Ryan. His gray eyes darkened like smoldering storm clouds. Maybe he wasn't so oblivious to the contact between them. "What I meant to say was, I can get this off by myself. But thank you, anyway."

He threw her a crooked smile. Now that her dress was all but slipping off her body, why didn't he leave?

"I'll just wait here while you change, in case you need me again. No need wandering the halls half-naked for help."

Half-naked. Her cheeks flushed with heat. The dress was completely open in the back, and she had her hands firmly pressed against her chest to keep it from dropping to the floor. "It's almost falling off me right now, Ryan. I hardly think I'll need any more assistance. But thank you for your help. Goodnight."

Hoping he'd grab a clue that she wanted to be alone to undress, she fled to the dressing area.

The satin nightgown. She had no other choice. It was either that or eat her sandwich naked. Bet Ryan would like that. The way his eyes had gleamed when he saw her in her wedding gown led her to believe there might be a spark of interest.

She pushed the thought aside. Ridiculous. Ryan McKay had never been interested in her. Why would he be? She was nothing like the women he escorted. Not even close.

Attempting to redirect her thoughts to her hunger, she removed her underthings and slipped the gown over her head. Unable to resist, she ran her hands down the cool satin. A quick glance in the mirror shocked her. The gown molded to her body like a lover's hand, clearly showcasing every minimal asset she had.

Why hadn't she heard the door close? Surely Ryan had left by now. Faith waited a few more seconds for the sound of the door closing, but didn't hear anything.

"Ryan?"

"Yeah?"

He was still there but his voice was muffled.

"What are you doing?"

"Eating."

"Oh." She peered around the doorway into the bedroom. He sat at the table next to her bed, eating one of the sandwiches Leland had fixed for her.

"You haven't eaten yet, Faith. Come out and have one of these sandwiches."

"No, that's okay. I'm not that hungry, really." Right. She was surprised Ryan couldn't hear her stomach grumbling in the other room.

"Don't be ridiculous. Come out here now and eat with me."

Fortunately the gown had a matching satin wrap that she quickly donned. Hunger won out over modesty. She wanted to get some food before he ate it all. She tightened the belt on the robe and entered the bedroom.

As she crossed in front of him, his eyes widened. Faith clutched the edges of the robe over her chest, feeling less than adequate in a gown that should have been worn by a goddess like Erica, not by her. She didn't do it justice.

"Hungry?" he asked.

Faith nodded. "Starving. I hadn't realized that I hadn't eaten until Leland mentioned something about food."

Ryan smiled. "I know. When I saw the food on the table my stomach reminded me I hadn't eaten since breakfast. You don't mind, do you?"

"Why would I mind?" She grabbed a sandwich and tried not to shove it in her mouth. With as much dignity as she could muster considering the depth of her hunger, she took a bite of the delicious turkey sandwich.

He sipped a glass of tea and watched her eat. At first she was self-conscious, but then her appetite took over and she downed the sandwich in no time flat.

Satisfied, Faith sat back and took a drink. And still he stared at her.

"Is something wrong?" She knew he wanted to say something, but didn't. She chewed her lip in anticipation.

Without a word he reached across the table and drew his thumb against the corner of her mouth, then slowly dragged it across her bottom lip. Faith watched in rapture as he brought his thumb to his mouth and licked it with agonizing slowness.

"You had mayonnaise on the corner of your lip," he said, his voice low and oh-so-sexy.

Was he deliberately trying to drive her crazy? She grabbed the napkin and swept it across her mouth. "Thank you."

His dark eyes warmed her. "It was my pleasure."

She couldn't tear her gaze away from him, despite knowing she should stop whatever was happening between them. She simply could not deal with any more today.

Thankfully, Ryan stood. "I'm sure you're tired. I'll let you get some sleep."

Faith rose from the table, nodding. "Thank you for your help with the dress."

"You're welcome," he said and stepped toward her, taking her hands in his. He pulled her against his chest and slid his arms around her back.

The crisp hairs of his chest rubbed her breasts. The thin silk of the gown and robe did little to keep the heat of his body from hers. Her nipples hardened against him, the rush of desire almost dropping her. Her limbs turned to gelatin and she felt weightless and lightheaded.

"Two months, Faith," he said softly as his head dipped towards her. "That's a very long time. Are you sure?"

This wasn't fair. No one had ever held her like this, made her feel such uncontrollable need. She wanted so much to experience these feelings, to step toward that desire and know what she hadn't known before. Blood pounded at her temples and liquid heat pooled deep within her. She was certain Ryan could sense her reaction because he tightened his hold on her, his hands softly kneading the muscles of her back, gradually sliding lower and lower.

"I...it's...you agreed to it." Pitiful excuse.

"I know. How stupid of me."

The smoke-filled depth of his eyes drew her in, hypnotizing her senses, rushing over her like a wildfire out of control.

If his lips drew any closer they'd touch hers. Faith was sure she'd die if they did. She was already losing control, inhaling his scent with rapid breaths, his hands burning against the silk of her gown, drawing her ever nearer to the heat of his lips.

Then just as suddenly as it started, the storming inferno was over. Ryan stepped back, his lips parted as the hint of a smile crossed his features.

"Tomorrow, you move into my bedroom. Goodnight, Faith."

He turned around and walked out, closing the door behind him.

Faith stood in the middle of the room, wondering what had just happened. Her breathing still hadn't returned to normal. The rhythm of her heart continued to pound its staccato beat. She still felt him, smelled him, all but tasted him on her lips as the memory of his thumb against her mouth singed her skin.

Despite her thoughts about needing to wait, wanting to wait, she had been ready to leap into her husband's arms.

She thought she had more self-control than that. It was obvious her inexperience was no match for the powerful charm of Ryan McKay. She'd have to be extra careful over the next couple months and try to keep her distance from him. Too much of his overpowering sexuality and she'd self-combust. Clearly, she was not ready at all for an intimate encounter with Ryan.

Two months wasn't nearly long enough.

And yet, two months was a very long time.

Ryan was irritated as hell as he pondered the papers he'd been reading when Faith had knocked at the door.

What had he been thinking? He hadn't intended to stay in her room and eat. And he sure hadn't intended to seduce her. Although it certainly seemed like she had been willing. And his main goal *was* to get her pregnant.

So why had he stopped? He'd had her, literally, ready to fall into bed with him. Her pupils dilated at his touch and when he pulled her against him her nipples hardened like tiny pebbles. With a little coaxing on his part, she might have agreed to making love.

God knows he'd been ready. The slightest touch of her skin had him aching. But instead of pressing his advantage, he had walked away.

Now that was a stupid move.

In business, when he saw an opening, he went for the throat. He should have done that with Faith. After all, it was the same as business. Everything had a goal. His goal with Faith was one, to marry her, which he'd done, and two, to get her pregnant, which he could have had a chance at tonight.

Was it because of her admission of being a virgin? He'd never had a virgin in his life, preferring the ease and comfort of well-experienced women. No attachments that way. He'd have to tread carefully with her.

Which was most likely why he'd backed away tonight. Helluva time to come up with scruples.

Maybe it was stupid, but he had discovered one thing tonight. They had chemistry. Loads of it. Besides gaining lifetime control of McKay Corporation, if nothing else would come of this marriage Ryan was certain some seriously great sex would be a part of it.

He didn't want for many things, but when he saw something he wanted, he did whatever it took to get it.

And he wanted Faith. Oh, he'd always thought her attractive, and her innocence and vulnerability only added to her allure. As his assistant, he wouldn't have considered it for a minute. As his wife, now that was different.

Tomorrow she'd move into his bedroom. Into his bed. Then it was only a matter of time. If the way she reacted tonight was any indication, it wouldn't take two months.

After all, two months was a very long time.

Chapter Four

Faith stretched and yawned, her body warm from the sunlight pouring in the windows next to her bed. For a moment she couldn't get a grasp around the dream she'd had. But as soon as she managed to open an eye, the realization hit her.

No dream. This was her new reality. She really was Ryan's wife.

She could lie in the bed all day until she figured out how to deal with the unfamiliarity of it all, or she could embrace the change as a new adventure.

Or possibly a combination of both. She threw off the covers and stepped to the window, admiring the beauty of the grounds outside.

A semi-circle of palm trees waved over the expertly manicured lawn. Brightly colored flowers and bushes offered a rainbow effect across the area. It really was lovely. She made a mental note to fully tour the house and grounds today and familiarize herself with the layout.

But first she had to get dressed and downstairs. It was already ten, much later than she usually slept. Despite the turmoil of yesterday she had slept like a baby. The bed was soft and comfortable, the sheets the same buttery satin as that of her gown.

She took a shower, dried her hair and bound it in a tight bun at the back of her neck.

But now a dilemma. What was she supposed to wear? Last night there had been nothing but the nightgown in the expansive closet. And she certainly wasn't leaving her room dressed in that.

Maybe she'd missed something. A pair of jeans or sweats. *Anything.*

She opened the closet, shocked to find several outfits hanging there. Neat stacks of lingerie lined the partially opened dressers. Someone must have put clothes in there while she was sleeping. She'd really been dead to the world not to be aware someone had come into her room.

At least she had something to wear. The cream linen pants and matching blouse didn't fit as loose as her usual clothes, but were still better than traipsing downstairs in a silk nightgown.

The kitchen was empty. She felt a momentary stab of guilt and hoped the staff wouldn't think she was the type to laze about in bed all day.

A pot of coffee caught her eye and she began a desperate search through the cabinets before finding the cups. She sat at the rectangular glass table and sipped her drink while perusing the outside through the large bay window.

Everything was foreign to her, from the flavored coffee to the view from the kitchen table. This would take some getting used to, but she refused to look on the situation with trepidation. More like a vacation—a really long vacation.

"You're awake."

Faith jumped at the sound of James McKay's voice and whirled around to find Ryan's cousin standing in the doorway.

James was a year younger than Ryan. They were both tall and wore their hair the same way, short and a little spiky on the top. James was different, though, mainly in attitude. Ryan was all business while James was all play.

Faith rarely saw him at the McKay offices. Ryan told her James was more interested in traveling, tennis and carousing than he was in actual work. But when the occasional social events occurred, he always managed to make an appearance.

"Good morning, James," she said, trying to be polite. Faith had never liked him. He was sickeningly sweet to the point of frightening her. The leering grins he threw her way made her want to scratch all over. Despite his overt friendliness, James McKay didn't have a sincere bone in his body. Faith knew the only reason he wanted control of McKay Corporation was because he hated Ryan. It had nothing to do with personal drive or ambition.

"I hear you married my cousin last night." James helped himself to coffee and sat in the chair next to Faith. "How did you manage that?"

What was she supposed to say? It was a known fact to almost everyone that the terms of Quentin McKay's will forced Ryan to marry, so James knew it wasn't a love match.

"Unfortunately, Erica could not marry Ryan, so he asked me to help him."

"And ever the faithful assistant you are, of course you couldn't say no." James cast a patronizing smile. He was plying her for information. She was bound and determined to give him nothing.

"Of course."

James circled his finger around his cup. "And the cheapskate didn't even take you on a honeymoon? He was planning to take Erica to Hawaii. I'd have thought he'd take you. I guess not, huh?"

She tried to ignore James's intended slam. So she wasn't Erica and was in fact Ryan's last and only hope to meet the terms of the will. Obviously he and Erica had quite a different relationship. That's why he hadn't taken Faith to Hawaii.

Not that she really wanted to go. Not much, anyway. Okay, she would have been delighted if he'd suggested it.

"We have work to do on Monday. Obviously, marrying me was quite different than marrying Erica."

"Obviously." James smirked.

No wonder Ryan didn't like him.

"So now I get to be your watchdog for the next year. I'm looking forward to that."

"I'll just bet you are," Ryan said as he walked into the kitchen.

Faith's eyes met Ryan's and he smiled as he headed toward her. She was shocked to the tips of her toes when he bent down and brushed a light kiss on the top of her head.

"Good morning, wife." His voice was low and warm.

Her eyes lingered on him. "Good morning," she finally managed in a throaty whisper that sounded more sensual than shocked.

"Well isn't this cozy? The newlyweds all warm and cuddly after their first night together." James leaned back in the chair and scrutinized them, arching one brow. "Must have been an eventful wedding night."

Oh God. Wedding night. Faith looked to Ryan in horror as she realized all her things were still in the other bedroom. The last thing they needed was for James to find out they hadn't spent their wedding night in the same room.

But Ryan had a calm Faith didn't possess. He lightly caressed the side of her neck with his fingertips. Despite the fact she knew this was for James's benefit only, her body responded, tightening and flooding with desire.

"Yes, it was an eventful night," he said in a husky voice that even Faith believed to be genuine.

"This looks like the right place." Stan Fredericks entered the kitchen.

Faith had always liked Stan. He had an open, honest face and was sharp as a tack in business matters. Plus, he was devoted to Ryan. As attorney to the McKay family, Stan had been around more than twenty-five years, and the McKays considered him a friend as well as business associate.

"You might as well join in," Ryan said. "James has already plied us with questions. Now it's your turn."

Stan grinned at Ryan, clearly unaffected by his client's surly tone. "I don't have any questions right now. Just stopped in to fulfill my official duties before I run off to play tennis. I'm having my things moved in this afternoon, so you can direct them to whatever bedroom you choose."

Ryan nodded and Stan left.

"This should be a fun year, all of us huddled up together like one big, happy family." James leaned back and crossed his arms, a satisfied smile on his face.

"Yeah. Right. Lots of fun," Ryan answered.

Ryan's clipped tone alerted Faith to his state of irritation. No one got under his skin more than his cousin.

"Well, I think I'll head on up to my bedroom and have a nap. I'll take the one down the hall from yours," James said with a yawn as he rose from the table.

Down the hall? But that was where she had slept last night. Where her things still were. Faith stood, ready to run upstairs if necessary. "Wait!"

James turned and lifted an eyebrow. "Something wrong with that bedroom?"

Ryan squeezed Faith's shoulder. "Not at all. My new bride thinks that maybe she'll make too much noise at night and keep you awake, being so close to our room."

Her cheeks flamed. James laughed.

"I'll be sure to keep my ears open for suspicious noises then," James said with a wink in her direction.

As soon as he left the room Faith turned to Ryan. "My things are still in there! My wedding dress and—"

"Don't worry," he said, placing his hands on her shoulders. "As soon as you left the bedroom the staff moved your things to my room, changed the sheets, made the bed and cleaned up the bathroom. It will look like no one's slept in that room in years."

Faith exhaled with relief. "Oh. That was close."

Ryan chuckled. "Not really. I already figured James would pop up earlier than expected. He may think he's smarter than me, but he's not. If you hadn't slept like the dead this morning I'd have had it done much sooner."

Guilt immediately set in. "I'm sorry, I'm usually an early riser. I don't know what happened. You should have woken me."

"Hey, relax. I was teasing you. You had a long day yesterday. I'm surprised you didn't sleep later."

She wasn't buying it. "You had a long day yourself, but I'll bet you didn't sleep in."

He shrugged. "I don't sleep much."

"Why not?"

"I just don't. I have lots to do and an equal amount of nervous energy to go along with it. I don't know, maybe I just don't know how to relax."

"You should try reading. It helps me relax."

"I read plenty."

Faith shook her head. "Not proposals and contracts, Ryan. Books. Fiction. For fun and pleasure."

He pulled an escaping tendril of her hair through his fingers. "I have something else in mind for fun and pleasure, and it doesn't involve reading."

With a quick step back, Faith grasped her coffee cup and headed toward the sink. "I'd like to take a look around the house and grounds today, if that's all right."

Ryan came up behind her and placed his cup in the sink. But instead of moving away he stayed put, his breath teasing the tiny hairs at the nape of her neck. He trailed a finger down the side of her neck. Certain she was going to collapse, she focused on breathing normally.

"I think you're avoiding the subject of sex," he teased, lightly blowing on her neck.

She felt the goose bumps trail down to her curling toes. "No, I'm not."

He grasped her shoulders and turned her around. "I agreed not to have sex with you for two months, Faith. I didn't agree not to talk about it."

The last thing on her mind was talking about it, thinking about it or experiencing it. Not now. The mere thought of being that close to Ryan melted her insides. The casual touches and glances he'd given her last night and this morning flamed a yearning she hadn't known existed. Right now that was all she could handle.

His body hovered inches from hers, his hands lightly stroking her arms. It wasn't *her* he wanted, she reminded herself. It was her body—a baby-making machine that would free him from the bonds of his grandfather's will. And that was all she'd ever be to him. To think anything else would be foolish.

"I can't right now, Ryan. We...we agreed to wait."

Ryan dropped his hands and stepped back. She turned around to face him now that he had given her some breathing room.

The warmth she expected to see, that she'd felt from his voice when he touched her, was gone. Had she hurt him with her rejection? How was she supposed to know what to do? This was unfamiliar territory, and she didn't know the ground rules.

"Fine. Look around," he said. "If you have questions, Leland will help you."

Faith nodded and Ryan walked away. She'd noticed his furrowed brow and knew he'd been disappointed. Now she felt guilty, although she didn't know why.

So many things to learn. That's why she needed time to figure out how she was supposed to act around him. Everything had changed yesterday—first the wedding, then last night. Both their lives would be different now.

She spent the rest of the morning wandering the house and grounds. It was truly a magnificent place, with five bedrooms and four bathrooms, each room larger than most people's apartments. At least larger than hers.

The staff had their own home adjacent to the main one, except for Leland and his wife Margaret, the head housekeeper. They stayed in the main house on the ground floor.

Faith found Margaret when she entered Ryan's bedroom— correction—their bedroom. Best not to think about that right now, although she knew she'd have to by tonight.

"Good morning, Mrs. McKay," Margaret said brightly. A petite woman in her early fifties, Margaret was friendly and welcoming. Faith had always liked Margaret. The woman didn't know how to frown. Perennially cheerful, she was the exact opposite of Leland's staid demeanor. Maybe that's why they made a good couple—they complemented each other.

"Good morning, Margaret," Faith said as she tentatively entered the room. "Just thought I'd pop in and take a look around."

"Of course you can. This is your room. I'm just straightening up in here. Would you like me to leave?"

Faith shook her head. "Not at all. Go ahead and continue what you were doing. And call me Faith, please."

Ryan's room was even larger than the one Faith slept in last night. A king-sized four-poster bed centered the room. The dressing area and bathroom were separate from the bedroom. Two oversized walk-in closets were positioned at opposite ends of the dressing area. Faith stepped into Ryan's, marveling at his collection of clothes, both business and casual. Which meant the other closet was hers. When she walked in, Margaret was hanging Faith's clothes.

"I didn't know my things had arrived," Faith said and picked up a couple hangers. "Let me help you."

Margaret looked horrified. "No, Mrs. McKay, I'll take care of it."

Obviously, Margaret wasn't going to call her by her first name, either. Despite the woman's continued protestations, Faith helped her unpack. It felt good to be doing something normal again, something familiar. It didn't take long anyway as Faith's wardrobe was fairly limited to her work suits and a few casual clothes.

When they were finished, Margaret left and Faith was able to explore the rest of Ryan's room.

There was a small sitting area to the left of the bed, with a plump, cushioned window seat built into a bay window. Two small lamps were mounted on the wall adjacent to the window. There was even a bookshelf nestled underneath the window seat, although it was empty.

Faith could already imagine herself relaxing in front of the window, reading and drinking a cup of tea. She sighed in pleasure at the thought. Reading was her passion, and she spent almost all her free time engaged in the fantasy world of someone else's life. Her favorites were romance novels, where the heroine found the man of her dreams, and despite trials and tribulations, always ended up happily-ever-after.

Not the way real life worked at all, which is why she loved to read them. At least her favorite characters found their soul mates.

But reading could wait for later. Right now she planned to enjoy the warm day and heated pool. She changed into her swimsuit, threw on a long sundress and headed outside.

It was blissfully warm as she opened the back door and stepped onto the covered patio. Fragrant flowers bloomed. Faith inhaled the sweet jasmine twining around the latticed arbor. Summer was coming, and despite the unpleasantly hot weather during those months, it was still her favorite time of year.

She couldn't wait to swim a few laps. A quick glance around showed no one about, so she dropped her sundress and dove in.

The water was perfect. One of her favorite things to do was head to the YMCA after work and swim to drive away the stress of the day. It was great exercise and never failed to rejuvenate her.

After several laps, she stopped in the center of the pool and floated on her back, enjoying the heat of the sun on her face and the utter quiet of being partially submerged in the silent water.

Ryan found Faith lying on her back in the middle of the pool, completely oblivious to the world around her. She barely moved, occasionally fluttering her arms or legs to maintain her balance as she allowed the sun to worship her body.

He had never seen her this close to unclothed before. Why in heaven's name did the woman hide under business suits two sizes too big and way too long? She had a magnificent body, perfectly proportioned. Sleek and athletic, with slender hips and slim legs. Trying to hide her figure under that ugly navy tank suit did no good. It still hugged her body like a sports car on a sharp curve.

He'd always had a thing for petite women, and Faith was small and perfect, right down to her pink-painted toenails. Cute. Incongruent in a woman who made trying to look plain an art form.

Her dark hair floated around all sides of her face, and he caught a tiny tinge of freckles across her cheeks and upturned nose. He wondered how long he could stand by the edge of the pool and watch her before she noticed he was there?

Why in the world was he even down here, and in his swim trunks? Ryan never took the time to swim. In fact, this was the first time in years he'd even contemplated taking a dip. His normal use for the pool was as decoration for social events held at the mansion.

But that was before he'd spotted the water nymph from his office window. Without thinking, he'd thrown on his swim trunks and made a mad dash for the pool.

Now that he was here, what was he going to do?

An idea popped into his head. He couldn't. It really wasn't a mature thing to do, and God knows it had been years since he'd done it. He still remembered the stern look on his grandfather's face when his golf partners had gotten wet. Ryan had received a thirty-minute lecture on propriety and acting like a child. But then again, he *had* been a child when it happened.

But there she was, looking calm and peaceful in the center of the pool, just begging for someone to splash her. He grinned.

Screw it. He was going in. Taking a few steps back, he ran toward the water, leaped high in the air and tucked both knees up to his chest. He hit the deep end with his first adult cannonball.

A good one, too. He landed on the bottom and quickly pushed off to the surface, throwing his head side to side to sluice the water out of his eyes before opening them.

In front of him stood one seriously drenched water nymph.

Faith spit water through hair that fell over her face. When she managed to pull the strands aside and cock one eye open, Ryan almost laughed at the picture she presented. Almost.

She blew the strands of hair out of her mouth. "You scared me half to death!"

He tried to keep his lips from curling. "Sorry, I couldn't resist."

"Well, next time try harder."

Ryan's eyes widened as he heard Faith complain for the very first time. In five years of working with her, he'd never heard a cross word or protest from her. At times she could be annoyingly agreeable, or at least if she had a differing opinion she diplomatically presented her case, but always accepted Ryan's decision as final.

Right now she looked pissed as hell. It certainly enhanced her appearance considerably, her small, high breasts heaving in indignation and her face bright with creamy color from the sun. She looked warm and lush and utterly delectable. He fought the urge to lick the droplets of water off every inch of her skin.

"If I promise to behave, will you stay and swim with me?" he asked.

"If I promise to stay and swim with you, will you promise not to act like an eight-year-old?"

It was all he could do not to laugh out loud at the sheer joy of the moment. He had been, in fact, eight years old the last time he'd tried the cannonball trick. And just now he'd felt that long ago childhood freedom as he'd sailed in the air before plummeting with glee into the safety net of the pool's depths.

"I'll try," he said, desperately trying to keep his smile in check.

"You do that."

She looked like a schoolteacher giving a lecture. Except she didn't look like any of the teachers he'd had, nor did her current appearance in any way reflect the way she presented herself at work. Without those owlish glasses to hide behind, her blue eyes sparkled like sapphires. Funny how they always seemed a duller blue behind her specs.

Her shoulders were thrown back, pushing her chest out. He liked the indignant look—especially when she pointed her erect nipples in his direction.

"Are you cold?" This time he couldn't fight the smirk.

Faith shook her head, seemingly confused. Then she followed his eyes to her chest and quickly wrapped her arms around her breasts.

Was she trying to hide her body from him? Hadn't she already adequately done that in that antiquated version of bathing attire?

"So, are you enjoying the pool?" he asked.

"I...um...I came down here to swim a few laps and read. Alone."

"Is that your not so subtle way of saying you'd like me to leave?"

A look of alarm crossed her face. "Oh, no! I mean, this is your house and your pool. I certainly wouldn't presume to tell you that you couldn't be anywhere you chose."

There was the always agreeable, prim and proper Faith. For a moment there he'd wondered where she'd gone when she'd turned into an oh-so-pissed-off bathing beauty. He'd enjoyed that small glimpse of spunk.

"I just wanted a quick dip, anyway." With a turn, he cut through the water and hoisted himself out. He grabbed a towel from the stack and dried himself. "I've got some work to do in the office downstairs tonight, so I probably won't surface until later. Leland will see that you get dinner."

"Okay."

Her gaze fell to the water, whether from disappointment or relief, he couldn't tell. She'd made it clear she didn't want him to stay, so why did she seem unhappy with the fact he was leaving?

"I tend to lose track of time when I'm working, so don't wait up for me. I'll probably come to bed late."

He waited for his words to sink in, and tried not to smile when she lifted her head, her eyes wary.

They might not be having sex, but they *would* be sleeping together. For some reason he wanted her as uncomfortable

71

about the situation as he was going to be, for entirely different reasons, of course.

Right now, she looked damned uncomfortable.

Satisfied, he turned toward the house.

Chapter Five

Don't wait up for me. Ryan's words stayed with Faith the rest of the day and well into that evening. She paced the expansive bedroom, casting frequent glances toward the clock on the bedside table. When she wasn't looking at the time, she was contemplating Ryan's bed. No, not Ryan's bed. *Their* bed. The one she had to share with him tonight.

She would *not* hyperventilate. She simply refused to let a simple thing like sleeping with Ryan cause her throat to go dry and her heart to run a marathon.

It was after midnight and still no sign of him. Did he think she'd just go to sleep, knowing that at some point he'd come in and slide under the sheets with her? Maybe it wasn't a big deal for him, but it was for her.

For a woman who'd barely had a handful of first dates her entire life, she'd certainly made some major leaps in the past couple days.

It wasn't like she had to have sex tonight. Their agreement was quite clear. All she was going to do tonight was sleep with him. Ryan had promised to honor her wishes for a little time, so there was no reason for her to panic. She should just relax and quit pacing a hole in the carpet.

Oh, right, like that was going to happen. The word *relax* wasn't even in her vocabulary.

She glanced at the king-sized bed, its pale amber coverlet pulled back. Her fingers traced an absent pattern over the satin sheets beneath.

Okay, no sex. But still, she'd be closer to a man than she ever had been before. A man who was also her husband. A man who, despite her bargain with him to wait, she'd eventually have sex with.

Forcing her breathing to slow down, she pushed away the queasy feeling, chalking it up to nothing more than a simple case of indigestion.

She was being ridiculous and naïve. It was time to grow up. She'd agreed to this marriage. It really wasn't a big deal. Besides, at twenty-six years old it was way past time she found out what she'd been missing all these years.

"What *have* you been missing all these years?"

She stopped dead in her tracks and turned to see Ryan at the doorway. His entrance sure made her breathing slow down. In fact, she was certain she'd stopped breathing altogether. Really, she must try to stop thinking out loud.

"And do you always talk to yourself?" He threw a stack of papers on the desk before stopping in front of her.

"Sometimes." Wonderful. Not only did he catch her talking about sex, but out loud. To herself.

"You didn't answer my question."

Didn't he ever look sloppy? Past midnight and he still looked fresh and oh-so-handsome. The black cashmere sweater accentuated the silvery glint in his dark eyes.

"What question?" she asked.

"What have you been missing all these years?"

"Oh, that one." The one she hoped he'd forget he'd overheard. Obviously not. "Did you get all your work finished?"

"Yes, I did, and you're avoiding my question." He slid his index finger down her arm.

Faith yawned. "Wow, look how late it is. I'm tired."

He smiled. "I'm surprised you're not already in bed. And you're still dressed."

After her shower, she'd been afraid to change into pajamas. Pajamas meant bed, and that she couldn't wrap her mind around just yet. She looked down at her too-big sweatpants and oversized sweatshirt. "Oh. I was reading and lost track of time."

"I see. Well, I agree with you. I'm beat. Think I'll take a shower and get ready for bed." He sat on the bed and removed his shoes.

As he headed into the dressing area Faith sat on the long brocade chaise against the wall, her head resting in her hands. How was she going to handle this? This intimacy, this sharing of personal space?

She paused as the sounds of running water and the shower door closing riveted her attention. A crystal clear image of Ryan naked popped into her head. He'd be turning his face to the shower spray, letting the steamy water sluice over his dark hair. He'd grab the soap and lather his hands, then run his palms over his chest and lower, until—

With desperate effort she tried to push the vision from her mind.

Said traitorous mind refused to cooperate. And then she heard new sounds. Beautiful, melodic sounds. She stepped closer to the door and listened.

It was Ryan. He was singing in the shower, his tenor voice perfect and unflawed. What was that song?

Oh, God. No wonder it was so familiar. He sang one of her favorite love songs, his clear, beautiful voice loud and sharp despite the running water.

"Ohhhh, my love, my darling, I hunger for your touch, this long, lonely night."

The haunting lyrics from "Unchained Melody" swept through her. Ryan's voice touched her as if his hands blazed a fiery trail from her trembling lips to her frantically beating heart.

He mesmerized her with his singing, capturing her in a spell. When he belted out "I need your love" at the top of his voice, her body melted. Without thinking she entered the dressing area, aching to step into the bathroom and listen to him, see him, touch him.

She hesitated.

So what stopped her? She was his wife. What would be the harm in going to him, in allowing him to touch her, to let him take her in his arms and kiss her, hold her like she'd waited her entire life to be held? To feel a man's touch, to finally experience a joining so intimate that poets struggled to find words to describe it.

She made it as far as the bathroom door, her hand on the knob, ready to turn it and fling open the gateway to the unknown. Then she remembered her mother's warning.

Don't ever fall in love, Faith. Men only want sex. If you give them your heart, they'll crush you and you'll never know a stronger pain.

Even years later those words influenced her, held her back, made her stop.

And look at you. You have no beauty—you're plain, just like me. Men will use and discard you like your father did to me.

She could already envision Ryan laughing at her. He was the picture of the perfect male. Gorgeous, intelligent, well-educated, able to pick and choose women of the highest caliber. Beautiful women, with social standing equal to his.

Instead, he had married his assistant. Not a glamour girl, or a socialite. Just plain and simple Faith. Not love, but a business deal.

She jerked her hand back from the doorknob and fled. As quickly as possible she donned her pajamas and retreated to the bedroom.

When Ryan stepped out of the bathroom Faith was sitting on the chaise. Her hands clenched the edge of the lounge like she was dangling from a cliff.

She looked terrified.

He'd never seen anyone so adorable in his life.

In her cotton pajamas with the long sleeves and legs and blue puffy cloud pattern, she looked like a frightened child. She'd pulled her hair back in a ponytail and chewed her lip nervously.

Ah yes, his calm, serene bride. The one with the death grip on the chaise.

Was he that imposing?

"I see you're ready for bed," he said.

She looked up, apparently finished with her examination of the carpet. She paled and looked like she might faint.

Now what was wrong? He had thrown on a pair of boxers instead of coming out of the bathroom stark naked as he was used to. Knowing Faith's intimacy issues, he hadn't wanted to give her a heart attack on their first night sleeping together.

So why did she look like she was about to jump out the window?

"Are you all right?" he asked.

She nodded.

"You sure?"

She nodded again.

"Shall we go to bed then?" It was like a game of charades. And he wasn't even being given hand signals for clues.

She didn't nod. She simply rose from the lounge like a prisoner heading for the guillotine and stood at the end of the bed.

"Well?" he asked.

"I was waiting to see what side you slept on so I could get in on the opposite side."

Ever the sacrificing one, wasn't she?

"What side do *you* sleep on?" he countered.

"The right."

Ryan slipped under the covers on the left side of the bed and held the blanket open for her. "Get in, then."

With agonizing slowness she lay down, turned her back and balanced precariously on approximately four inches of the bed. As far away from him as possible.

Ryan propped himself up on his elbow and watched her try to get into a sleeping position. If he didn't think he'd scare her out of her wits he'd have laughed. As it was, he was almost afraid to breathe for fear she'd bolt right up, or worse, fall off the bed.

It was like having an ironing board in bed with him. She was barely breathing and sure as hell wasn't moving. And he could swear the bed shook. Was she cold? Or just scared to death?

At least he couldn't take it as an insult for being lousy in bed. Unless criticism applied to simply sharing the space.

"Good night, Faith." Ryan reached up and turned off the light over his side of the bed. And waited.

"Night, Ryan," she finally answered, so quiet he barely heard her.

He rolled over onto his back and stared at the moonlit ceiling.

He wasn't in bed with a sixteen-year-old, that much was certain. Faith was old enough to know some things, even if she was a virgin. And it wasn't as if he'd told her he was planning to attack her their first night together.

They weren't strangers, either, so she should know he always kept his word. His word, in business, was as good as a written contract. And Faith knew that.

So what about him frightened her? Was it even him? Her fear was completely unnatural given the circumstances. He'd already agreed to give her two months.

Something else bothered her, something that made her so afraid that he knew if he suggested she camp out on the bedroom floor she'd have jumped at the chance.

He meant to find out what it was.

CB

It hadn't been at all like Faith thought it would be. The closer it got to bedtime, the more she'd hyperventilated. Why she'd been so afraid she had no idea, but it turned out her fears were groundless.

She had prepared herself for Ryan's attempts to convince her to have sex. Okay, maybe she could have been persuaded, if she could avoid leaping out of her skin should he touch her.

But she needn't have worried. Within twenty minutes she'd heard his deep breathing and knew he was asleep.

Then she'd finally exhaled. And tried to ignore the stab of disappointment.

What an idiot. First she'd been scared to death he'd touch her. And now, she was upset because he hadn't? What did she want from him?

If only she knew.

At least by the second night she wasn't as panic-stricken as she had been the first, knowing he wouldn't be pouncing on her the minute she got into bed.

This time, she hadn't balanced on the edge like a tightrope walker. And she'd actually managed to sleep.

Good thing, too, because today they'd head back to the office, those first awkward nights almost a distant memory already. The rest of the weekend she'd hardly seen Ryan, only for meals and at bedtime. He'd locked himself in his office claiming paperwork, but she knew it was because he really had no idea what to do with a wife around.

At least they'd have work to do today. By the time she'd awakened this morning, Ryan had already dressed and left the bedroom. Whether that was his usual routine or he'd done it as a courtesy to her, she didn't know. Either way she dressed and readied herself in a hurry, then went downstairs to find him sitting at the table, reading the newspaper and finishing breakfast.

"Good morning," she said, taking a seat and smiling her thanks when Margaret brought her a cup of coffee.

"Morning," he mumbled from behind the *Wall Street Journal.*

Now *that* was the Ryan she knew. The one who rarely looked up from whatever document he was engrossed in to even acknowledge her presence. Aloof, businesslike Ryan she could handle.

She rose to fix herself breakfast, but Margaret glared at her and told her to sit down.

The thought of other people doing things for her didn't seem right, but she sat at the table. "I can cook, Margaret, and I'm sure you have other things to do."

Margaret shook her head. "The lady of the house does not cook. That's *my* job."

"But..." She was about to protest but stopped when Ryan's hand lightly touched hers. He had put the paper down and crooked a smile at her, shaking his head.

"Don't bother arguing with Margaret," he said. "She's vicious and always gets her way."

"I heard that," Margaret said over the sound of sizzling bacon. Margaret threw a glance over her shoulder at Ryan, who winked at her. Faith caught the housekeeper's grin before she turned back to her cooking.

Interesting. Faith hadn't thought Ryan had feelings for anyone. Apparently she'd been wrong about that. His relationship with Margaret seemed close, almost like parent and child.

They rode to the office in Ryan's car but didn't speak. He started his business day early and spent the entire time on the phone.

"What will you be telling everyone at the office?" she asked when he ended his call.

"About what?"

"About us. Don't you think when everyone left on Friday they'd expect you'd be on your honeymoon today instead of coming back to the office? And that you'd be married to Erica, not me?"

Ryan didn't answer.

"You don't even have to tell anyone you married me," she said. "I certainly understand that you wouldn't want anyone to know."

He frowned. "Why wouldn't I want anyone to know?"

"That's quite obvious, don't you think?"

"Not to me."

Was he going to force her to say it? "Because you married me. Not Erica, not one of your friends. Me."

He swerved into a fast food parking lot, threw the car into park and turned to her. "And?"

"I'm merely stating the obvious. I'd like to know how you wish me to handle the inevitable questions."

"Tell anyone who asks that Erica backed out and you were gracious enough to marry me."

He had to be kidding. "Excuse me?"

"You heard me."

"You want me to *tell* everyone that I was gracious enough to marry you."

"Yes."

Right. Promptly followed by their hysterical laughter. "They'll ask questions. They'll want to know why."

"If they want more information than that, tell them it's none of their damn business. And if they still persist, then let me know and I'll handle it in a way I'm certain they won't care for."

He accelerated out of the parking lot and continued the drive to work. That was it. End of discussion. She was supposed to tell all the employees and all of his business associates that he had married her.

And then offer no explanation other than *none of your business.*

Sometimes he made her job difficult.

"Besides," he added, "Everyone at the hotel saw us Friday night. We did get married there, remember? By now, they all know."

Of course, he was right. She cringed at the thought and wondered what kind of reception she'd get when they showed up at work together.

CB

They were greeted by thunderous cheers and applause as they entered the office. Faith was stunned. Ryan had been right. Everyone knew.

Her desk was littered with cards and congratulatory banners, paper wedding bells and confetti. She tried to mask her thrill but couldn't help the silly giggle that escaped. What fun!

How much of everyone's enthusiasm was sincere and how much was due to the employees' attempts to kiss up to Ryan she didn't know, and frankly didn't care. It beat the cold stares or laughs she had expected to receive.

Ryan tolerated it for about fifteen minutes before he placed his hand on Faith's shoulder, lightly squeezing. She turned her head in his direction and he placed a soft kiss on her cheek, completely surprising her. And eliciting more applause from the crowd.

"I have some calls to make so I'll leave them in your capable hands," he whispered before retreating to his office and closing the door.

She spent a few more minutes socializing and then begged everyone to let her tackle the mound of paperwork on her desk. In a few minutes they were gone.

Faith smiled and sighed as she sat at her desk and twirled the large diamond ring around her finger. It wasn't at all as bad as she expected. Everyone had been nice.

At least no one had laughed in front of her. But later, when she wasn't around, she was certain the gossip would begin.

෨

"Do you think he was drunk that night?"

"Who knows? He would have to be to marry *her*."

Ryan stopped at the doorway to the kitchen.

"She's so dowdy. And what's with those ugly suits she wears?"

"And that hair, can you imagine? It looks like a bird's nest."

"Well the bird's nest goes with those glasses. They make her look like an owl."

Laughter erupted as the gossip continued. With every word, Ryan's blood pressure rose. He hated gossip. It was malicious, cruel, and often overheard by the person being discussed, leading to very hurt feelings.

This time they weren't discussing him. God knows he'd heard employees talking about him before, and it just rolled off his back. He was the head of the company, and was used to making decisions that someone didn't like, which invariably led to the staff bitching about him.

But these people were talking about his wife. And he didn't like it one damn bit.

"I'll bet he has to put a bag over her head to sleep with her."

That got the crowed laughing madly.

And was the straw that broke the boss's back. He'd had enough.

As soon as he entered the kitchen, all laughter and conversation halted.

"Afternoon everyone," he said, trying to sound cheerful. Inside, he was seething. He'd almost stepped in and blasted them, but decided on a different tactic.

Ryan fixed his coffee, making sure to take his time. Then he turned to them.

"I wanted to tell you all how much it meant to Faith to be received so well this morning."

Uneasy smiles filled the room.

"She was so nervous about what everyone would think. I told her not to worry at all, that McKay employees were the best of the best and would be more than happy about our marriage."

People shifted in their chairs.

"It's nice to know I wasn't wrong in that assessment. I was afraid some people would be jealous of Faith, or even make nasty comments about our marriage and the reasons for it. But I know that you all see in her what I've always seen."

More uncomfortable stirring. Staring out the windows, looking at the floors.

"Her kindness. Her intelligence. The way she accepts everyone regardless of their position." His gaze scanned the room. "Or their looks. Damn, am I a lucky man or what?"

No comments. A few nods and murmurs of agreement.

"Have a nice lunch, everyone." Ryan took his cup and walked out of the kitchen whistling.

He smiled all the way back to his office. Now that was fun.

Bunch of worthless gossips. He made a mental note to have employee evaluations conducted as soon as possible. It was time for a weeding out.

Sometimes it was good to be the king.

Chapter Six

"We're doing what?" Faith asked.

"Going shopping." Ryan noted her crossed arms and stubborn stance. This was going to be a battle.

"Why?" she challenged.

"Faith, do we have to argue about this? I thought all women loved to go shopping." Ryan leaned against the door to their bedroom's dressing area, completely flabbergasted at his wife's reluctance to shop.

"This one doesn't."

He could have laughed at the way she looked, her lips pressed firmly together and her eyes squinting in stubborn accusation.

"Why not?"

"I don't need anything." She'd already dismissed the idea and headed into their bathroom to pull her hair into that god-awful bun she wore.

"So?" He followed, determined to convince her.

"So why go shopping if I don't need to buy anything?"

Never in his life had he needed to convince a woman to spend his money. Was Faith from another planet?

Time to change tactics.

"I need to buy a few things, and I'd like you to go with me."

She stopped, her hands tangled in her hair and turned to look at him. "Oh. Okay."

Truthfully, the last thing in the world Ryan wanted to do on a Saturday was go shopping. But after spending the week mulling over the office gossip, he'd grown more irritated. Every time he thought about how they'd judged Faith based on her looks, he was more determined than ever to show them how wrong they were.

So he decided Faith needed a little change in her attire. Not that *she* needed to change. But after pondering the staff's comments, he wondered how much of what they said was a reflection of how she felt about herself.

Did she see herself as unattractive and plain? Did she dress that way deliberately in order to bury her insecurities?

Somewhere underneath that spinster getup was a beautiful butterfly, and Ryan intended to unwrap the cocoon.

Cʒ

This wasn't at all the shopping trip Faith had imagined. They'd ended up at Saks Fifth Avenue, in the Women's Department.

"I didn't know you wore women's clothes." She cast him a suspicious glare.

"I didn't know you hid a sense of humor under all those baggy things you wear."

"I'm not hiding anything," she said, adjusting the hips of her loose jeans and pulling the hem of her shirt down past her hips. "I like these clothes."

"Yes, they look...uh...comfortable, to say the least. However, now that you're my wife I'd appreciate if you'd indulge me and let me buy you a few things appropriate for Mrs. Ryan McKay."

She couldn't very well argue with that. The last thing she wanted to do was embarrass Ryan. She let him drag her to the designer boutique. The place was virtually empty except for two eager saleswomen who promptly gushed over Ryan while directing disapproving looks in Faith's direction.

"My wife needs a new wardrobe," he said to the ladies who identified themselves as Margo and Marie.

"Obviously," Margo replied, looking down her nose at Faith.

And these women made their living in sales?

Margo was in her early forties, her blonde hair swept up into a stylish twist. Marie was a twentyish version of Margo, with moonlit blonde hair and a body that could easily grace the centerfold of most men's magazines.

"What would you like to see?" Margo asked Ryan, apparently already grabbing a clue as to who held the credit card.

"Everything. Start with the basics and then work your way up. Business, casual and social, along with accessories."

Both women's eyes lit up like they'd just been given a Christmas bonus. They each took hold of one of Faith's elbows and steered her in the direction of the dressing room. She turned her head to shoot Ryan a pleading look. He smiled and waved, then picked up the remote control to the television in the waiting area. She'd already been forgotten.

In no time at all the women had evaluated her. She felt like she was about to be sold at auction. Margo spoke and Marie took notes.

"Five foot two, thirty-four B, twenty-four-inch waist, thirty-five-inch hips, thirty-inch inseam. Definitely a size four and petite."

Four? Petite? Who were they talking about? Surely not her. Bad enough to be standing there in nothing but her panties and bra, let alone being inventoried. Why in the world had she agreed to this?

"The first thing that has to go is that horrid cotton underwear."

What? This was not an underwear fashion show, and she was as undressed as she was going to get. She had let them poke and measure her, but she was standing firm on this one. The underwear stayed right where it was.

But she'd underestimated their power of persuasion. In the blink of an eye they had convinced her to squeeze into a flimsy, black silk chemise. It was one piece with a push-up bra that, even to Faith's eyes, gave her cleavage. It clung to her hips and rode high in the back.

"It's too small." She looked in the mirror and tried to tug what little fabric there was over her hips. The darn thing clung so tight she couldn't breathe. She preferred her underwear, like her clothes, to fit more loosely.

"It hugs your body perfectly. Wait until your husband sees you in that."

Not in a million years.

At last they brought clothes for her to try on over the scandalous lingerie. Every outfit was too small. Faith argued with both women for over ten minutes, steadfastly refusing to put on a single piece of clothing that wasn't her usual size.

Margo frowned at her. "You're a petite size four, Mrs. McKay, *not* three sizes larger."

"That's the size I usually buy, and it fits."

"Of course it fits. If there were two of you wearing the clothes it would still fit."

She burned with the need to stick out her tongue at Margo, but she tamped down the childish urge and lifted her chin. "I'm not trying any of those clothes on. It's a waste of my time and yours. They won't fit."

"We'll see about that," Margo replied before flouncing off in a huff. Marie stood in the dressing room preventing Faith's escape, her arms crossed in front of her chest and a smug look on her flawless face.

Faith released a sigh. Margo was going to get the correct sizes for her. Her sigh turned to a gasp when she came back with Ryan in tow.

There was nowhere to run and absolutely no place to hide. She didn't even have her own clothes as those vicious saleswomen had removed them from the dressing room. The women smiled and left her alone with Ryan.

Alone with her husband, and there she was in nothing but some black, lacy handkerchief.

Ryan stood there, mouth agape, and looked her over from head to toe. His eyes burned smoky and hot as his gaze took in her breasts, hips and legs.

Short of using the chair as clothing, she had nothing to cover herself with except her own hands. This was the most embarrassing thing that had ever happened to her.

"Wow," he rasped, his eyes raking over her.

Ready to self-combust in agonizing embarrassment, Faith could do nothing but stand inspection under his heated gaze.

Ryan cleared his throat. "Margo said you were having a disagreement about sizes."

Willing herself to disappear, she heaved a sigh. "There is no disagreement. I know what size I wear."

A feminine hand slipped through the door and handed Ryan a dress. He took it and stepped toward her.

"Why don't you try this on?" He handed Faith the black dress that she'd already told the women would never fit.

She grabbed it and held it in front of her, grateful at least for its blanketing abilities. "It's the wrong size."

"I'll make a deal with you. Put it on. If it fits, you agree to try on the rest of the clothes. If it doesn't, I'll have Margo take all these back and bring the size you want."

Now he was making sense. She nodded and waited for him to leave. He didn't.

"I said I'd try it on," she said.

"Do it now."

With a frustrated sigh, she stepped into the dress, turning her back so he could zip it up.

He slipped the zipper up in one easy move and Faith turned around to look in the mirror.

Dear God. That was *her* body? The dress fit like it was part of her skin, hugging every curve. It was made of the softest silk and cashmere, with long, tight-fitting sleeves. And instead of ending at her calves like her usual clothes, it stopped at mid-thigh, making her legs look long and slender instead of short and pudgy.

"Wow," Ryan commented.

He stood behind her and assessed her from her face to her feet.

"Wow," he said again.

He seemed to like that word a lot. Admittedly, she felt the same way as she perused herself in the mirror. And she'd never once in her entire life said *wow* about her own reflection.

Their eyes met and lingered. The dressing room suddenly seemed to shrink.

"That dress fits, Faith. Perfectly."

She couldn't believe, wouldn't believe that was actually her in the mirror.

"Look how it hugs your shoulders and arms, dips in the waist and swells out over your hips." He trailed his hand lightly down her arms, circling her waist briefly before caressing her hips and lingering there.

Her breathing stilted as she tried to control her body's response to his touch. His hands lazily clenched her hips, drawing her subtly against the front of him. Her butt connected with his hips and she sucked in a surprised breath at the sizzling contact.

She watched them in the mirror, his large hand squeezing and releasing the flesh at her hips. She knew he could feel her rapid inhalations against his chest, but for the life of her she couldn't regulate her breathing. Not when he touched her like that.

"This dress was made for you," he murmured, his breath warm as it ruffled against her neck. "You look gorgeous."

He had her, and he knew it. So did she.

"I...I guess the size is right after all. You can go get Margo and I'll try on the rest."

He didn't let go of her quite yet, seeming to enjoy running his hands over her. The evidence of how much he enjoyed it pressed hard against her lower back. She inhaled and held her breath, suspended in time, not wanting this moment to end. No man had ever looked at her the way Ryan did, with pure, unadulterated heat in his gaze. If she was at all experienced, she'd know what to do about that. But since she wasn't, all she could do was stare back at him, wishing she were a different person—more worldly, so she could take him up on the promise in his eyes.

Faith's legs wobbled. Could Ryan feel her trembling?

With a sigh, he stepped back and walked out of the room, dissolving the spell. And then she could breathe again. Damn, but the man did strange things to her. Her pulse raced so fast it took a moment for the world to right itself. And all he'd done was look at her.

What was going to happen when they made love?

She wasn't certain she'd live through the experience.

The masochistic saleswomen returned and subjected her to severe clothing torture. From work suits to dresses for both casual and social events, she was certain she had tried on every single item on the third floor. All in the size Margo picked. And from designers she'd only read about in women's fashion magazines.

Then she was required to parade herself in front of Ryan so he could see each outfit. She could tell which ones he liked because his eyes lit up and he cast her that smoldering look she was growing uncomfortably familiar with. The man had great taste. Every outfit she loved, he loved. The ones she cringed at the thought of wearing brought no spark from his eyes.

When she was certain they were through with the fashion show, the women brought out the accessories. Lingerie in every style and fabric, multiple colors and patterns. Bras, panties, garters, stockings, bustiers, chemises, slips and nightgowns. Faith had to choose the ones she liked while trying to think of anything but the fact that her husband might see her in them.

By the time they moved to shoes and handbags, trying different ensembles to go with different outfits, she was ready to scream from exhaustion.

When the ordeal ended, Faith went to change back into her old clothes.

"Mr. McKay informed us that you get to choose which of these to wear," Margo said.

Spread before her were her old clothes, plus a short, black, body-hugging skirt and a white silk blouse with matching lingerie. And of course, complementary shoes.

Now what? Clearly, Ryan had taken her on this expedition to buy her a new outfit. She'd hurt his feelings if she reappeared in her old, loose clothing. After all, he'd gone to all this trouble and had patiently waited while she tried on all the clothes.

With a last, longing glance at her comfortable clothes, she chose the new outfit, receiving a gush of praise from Margo.

She emerged from the dressing room and found Ryan at the sales register with Margo.

"Have them delivered by tonight," he instructed as he signed the sales slip.

"Absolutely," Margo replied, barely able to keep her smile from taking over her annoyingly perfect face.

When they walked away, Faith tugged Ryan's arm. "How many of those outfits did you buy?"

"Just a few."

Admittedly, the clothes felt wonderful. They weren't baggy like her clothes normally were, and she felt somewhat scandalous wearing the super short skirt. But she also felt good. Very good. Like maybe she was even dressed in style.

Still, she was thankful the ordeal was over.

They had lunch at the store's trendy bistro, and Faith hadn't realized how hungry she was until the waiter placed her shrimp salad in front of her. All that shopping had worked up an appetite. And extreme exhaustion. She'd be glad to go home.

But Ryan had another surprise for her. After lunch they headed downstairs. Instead of leaving the store, he led her to the hair salon.

This couldn't be happening.

They were greeted by the owner of the salon, a tall, thin, very enthusiastic man named John, who apparently had been expecting them.

"You must be Faith," John said, taking her arm and leading her into the salon. He squinted as he examined her bound-up hair, then turned to Ryan. "This may take several hours."

"Fine," Ryan said as he handed John his card. "Call my cell phone when you're done."

Before she could utter a word, Ryan had left and John led her to his chair, chattering on about how they *must* do something with her nest of hair.

They discussed hairstyles, and she resisted. They talked about highlights, and she balked. But John was relentless and Faith was tired. Truthfully, his suggestions had some merit. She'd needed a haircut for quite awhile, but had put it off as frivolous. Who was going to see her hair, anyway? And who would care? But now that John held her prisoner in his salon, maybe something new wouldn't be a bad idea.

For the next two hours she endured coloring, cutting, shampooing, blow drying and waxing. She'd been subjected to almost every form of cruel torture John and his crew could think of. This was how women got glamorous?

But when he'd finished and turned her towards the mirror, her mouth opened in shock.

Who was that woman staring back in the mirror? Surely, not her.

John had cut her long, thick hair to shoulder length. He'd given her wispy bangs that brushed her eyebrows, which were two now instead of one. So that's what the wax was for.

And instead of her dull brown color, he had added subtle highlights that made her sable hair shine against the light. He told her it would only take a few minutes to fix her hair each day. He also warned her if she continued to twist it up in an unsightly bun she'd most likely be bald by the time she was thirty-five.

Faith threw John a dubious look but he stared her down effectively. Okay, then. No more buns. She no longer had long enough hair to pull into a bun anyway.

It was amazing what a little makeup could do for her. Vanessa, the girl who did her makeup, said her face had a natural beauty, which Faith surmised was her way of getting a big tip. Vanessa showed her how to apply a small amount of eye shadow, mascara and a hint of blush to bring out the creamy color in her complexion.

Faith had to admit the girl worked wonders. She didn't look made up or glamorous, just natural. And, almost attractive. Sort of. But then again she was at a beauty salon, where they could make even the homeliest woman seem passable.

Faith waited for Ryan at the reception area. When he returned, he walked right past her to the counter. Maybe she had been hidden in the corner too much and he hadn't noticed her. She watched as he paid John and then looked around.

"Where's my wife?" he asked John.

As if he'd just created life from dead body parts, John swept his hand to Ryan's left. "Right in front of you."

Ryan turned and his eyes opened wide. Faith stood as he approached her, feeling suddenly nervous.

He didn't say anything, just cocked his head to the side and looked at her. Faith felt her face warm under his scrutiny.

Ryan didn't like the way she looked, it was obvious. His eyebrows knit together as if he were trying to figure out a complicated puzzle.

"You're stunning," he said, his eyes alight with pleasure.

Try as she might she couldn't hold back the smile, nor the tears that threatened.

"Thank you."

He reached toward her face and plucked her glasses off before she could utter a protest.

"Do you really need these to see?"

She tried not to meet his eyes as she pondered the walls of the salon. "Sort of."

"What does that mean?"

"I do need them, but only for reading."

"Then why do you wear them all the time?"

"I don't know. So I don't lose them?"

Ryan shook his head and folded her glasses, tucking them into her purse. "You don't need them to walk with me. Come on."

He grabbed her hand and they walked silently out of the store. Faith stole glances at Ryan's profile. His brows knit together in that familiar way. Was he annoyed?

Now what? He didn't like the way she looked, that was it.

This whole makeover thing hadn't been her idea anyway. She'd been happy with the way she was before. Her clothes, her hair, everything. She hadn't wanted to change anything—he had.

She worried her bottom lip as she thought about why he'd be unhappy. Maybe it was disappointment. Maybe he thought she'd turn into this raving beauty, only to find she wasn't any different than before. Oh, he'd been nice to her by telling her she was stunning, but he was probably being more polite than honest.

He'd gone to all this trouble today, only to discover she wasn't changeable.

Her mother had always reminded her of that old saying, *You can't make a silk purse out of a sow's ear.* Faith didn't really care for the sow's ear idea, but she certainly was no silk purse.

They arrived home a short time later and Ryan headed into his office and closed the door. Faith endured the house staff's fawning and telling her how lovely she looked, knowing they were simply being polite. She thanked them, then escaped to the safety of her room to be alone.

For the longest time she stood in front of the full length mirror reviewing her new clothes and appearance. She shook her head and walked away.

Some things were better left unchanged.

 C%

Ryan tried for the fifteenth time to read the newest proposal for improvements and expansion at the hotel, but he couldn't concentrate on business.

Instead, his mind wandered to the incredibly beautiful brunette he'd married. Her hair shined like mink and her crystal blue eyes sparkled like. diamonds. And those shapely legs teased him, peeking out under the sinfully short skirt she'd worn home from the store.

He dropped his head in his hands and rubbed his temples. What had he done?

When he'd seen her at the salon, he'd felt an instant rush of heat that almost knocked him down. The transformation had been incredible. All he really wanted to do was give her a little lift, make her feel better about herself, and quiet the gossips at the office who'd insulted her.

Instead he'd played Frankenstein and created a monster. A petite, gorgeous monster who threatened to turn him into a raving sex maniac right in the middle of the hair salon.

It was all too much. First, trying to have a normal conversation in the dressing room while she'd been wearing that hot and sexy black underwear had him hard and in agony instantly. Then, that dress she'd tried on molded to her every curve and he'd wanted to strip her naked and make love to her right then and there.

The moment his gaze had settled on her at the salon, he'd wanted to pull her against him and drag his fingers through her silky hair, grasp it in his hands and pull her mouth against his. He'd fought the raging urge to ravage her full lips with hot kisses and snake his hands over her body and down those luscious legs until...

Until what? Obviously, he couldn't have done any of those things in public. But he'd wanted to. God, how he'd wanted to.

Well, now he'd done it. He'd made his wife desirable. More so than she already had been. At least before it had been subtle. Now, she stood right out there. And he had almost two months to wait before he could make love to her.

He shifted uncomfortably in his chair. He was aching and hard and using every ounce of restraint he possessed to keep from going to her and putting an end to this ridiculous wait. His body pulsated with the need to cover her body with his, to drive into her moist heat and feel the agonizing pleasure of releasing inside her.

He raised his head, suddenly shocked at where his thoughts had drifted.

He needed to get her pregnant. That was it. Not because he desired her. He didn't have those kinds of needs. This was a physical thing only. And a business arrangement. Nothing more.

But, he had almost let it get personal. And getting involved with Faith, with any woman for that matter, went completely against his standards. No way was he going to fall in love. Ever.

He'd been personal witness to the havoc created by so-called love, and wanted no part of it.

So, something had to change. Ryan had to convince Faith to have sex with him sooner. He needed to get her pregnant so he could leave her alone, stop thinking about her, stop wanting her.

It was a simple matter, really. Ryan was an expert at getting women into bed. And Faith was a woman, just like any other. All he had to do was set a plan in motion and it would be only a matter of time until she leaped into bed with him, thereby satisfying both his physical desires and his business needs.

Seduction. Ryan tapped his pencil against the desk and formulated a plan, smiling when it came to him.

In no time at all he'd have Faith in his bed, and then quickly thereafter out of his thoughts.

Round one was about to begin.

Chapter Seven

It didn't take long for the men to come crawling out of the woodwork.

Ryan peeked outside his door. Faith worked away, oblivious to the number of guys strolling up and down the hallway. Dressed in her well-tailored black Armani suit and matching pumps, she was the epitome of fashion.

The blue silk blouse brought out the sapphire of her eyes. The silk stockings and three-inch heels made her legs stand out like they never had before. Especially since the skirt of her suit ended a few inches above her knee.

She oozed style, class and elegance.

Gone was the plain wallflower, and in its stead a beautiful, desirable butterfly.

Ryan hadn't realized how many butterfly hunters populated his executive offices. Men who hadn't left their desks in months suddenly found reasons to stroll by Faith's office, stopping to say hello and tell her how nice she looked.

Did they think he wouldn't notice?

Faith didn't pay any attention to them. Whenever someone came by, she smiled, engaged in minimal conversation and then resumed her work.

Didn't she know these guys were hitting on her?

On *her*. His wife. The woman who was taken, unavailable, married. To him.

Okay, so they were married in name only. But the guys sniffing around her didn't know that. And he didn't like them ogling her. In fact, he was downright pissed off about it.

Maybe he'd send out a memo.

He cringed at his wandering thoughts. He could see it now.

Memo to all male members of executive staff: Stop looking at my wife. She's mine. Mine, mine, mine, mine, mine.

Yeah, that would be professional, not to mention mature.

Disgusted, he tossed his paperwork aside and stepped to the doorway for the fifth time in the past half hour. Faith glanced up and smiled.

"Did you need something?" she asked.

Yes. I need you. Naked. In my office, on my desk, right now. "No, thanks." He turned and went back to his desk.

This was ridiculous. He was losing it, acting like a lovesick schoolboy. And where the hell had this possessive streak come from? It wasn't like him at all to care whether a woman he was dating was getting hit on by another guy.

Then again, Faith wasn't a woman he was dating. She was his wife.

In name only.

He really hated that voice inside his head right now.

This had to stop. It was time to put his plan into action.

Faith found Ryan's behavior very odd. She wasn't sure what was bothering him, but lately he'd been shadowing her like a personal bodyguard.

It couldn't be because he was attracted to her. She'd already surmised his disappointment was that her transformation hadn't turned out the way he'd hoped. But still, she went along with the new hairstyle and wardrobe.

Not that she'd had a choice. By the time they'd returned from shopping that day all her old clothes were missing, replaced by a closet full of almost everything she'd tried on at Saks. And Margaret was tight-lipped about where her old clothes had gone.

So she wore the new ones and had to admit, enjoyed them. They were lighter weight than what she used to wear, and lifted her spirits considerably. She loved putting on the different styles and textures, luxuriating in the feel of silk against her skin, or cashmere brushing up against her neck.

Despite the fact she now wore designer clothes and no longer put her hair up in a bun, nothing else had changed.

Interestingly enough, the office staff paid more attention to her now. Especially the guys. Faith had no idea what to make of that. Maybe they were buttering her up and being nice to her because she was married to the boss and they didn't want to get on her bad side.

She didn't have a bad side. Nor had she ever paid any attention to the men before. And certainly not now.

Marriage in name only or not, she *was* married. She took her vows seriously, even if her marriage wasn't a real one. And she wouldn't entertain notions of any other men. She could barely figure out what to do with the one she married.

"Faith."

Ryan peered out of his office. Again. "Yes?"

"We have a business dinner tonight at Markham's Restaurant. Eight o'clock. I'd like you to accompany me. Paul Worthington is bringing his wife, Jenelle."

Faith nodded. "All right, I'll make a note of that."

A business dinner. Her first social event as Ryan's wife.

Her stomach fluttered at the thought of going out in public as Ryan's wife. She hoped she'd handle herself appropriately. At least she had something decent to wear.

Faith showered and changed into a soft beige Chanel dress with a scoop neck, accentuated with a wide gold belt at the waist. She slipped on matching shoes and wound her hair up in a twist, leaving several tendrils escaping at the side of her face.

She had to admit the look worked. Since her new haircut, she'd bought a couple fashion magazines and played with some loose and easy styles for her new, shorter hair, just for a change of pace. The upsweep looked, well, elegant.

But underneath the clothes and hair was the same old Faith. *You can change the packaging as much as you want, but the product remains the same.*

"Are you ready?" Ryan stepped out of the dressing area, impeccably attired in a black suit, simple white shirt and designer tie.

Faith sighed. "Yes."

His eyes traveled the length of her body, warming her from the inside out. His lips quirked into the hint of a smile.

"You look very nice," he said in a voice so deep it vibrated her nerve endings.

"Thank you."

They started for the door but Ryan stopped her. "Wait a second, I forgot something." He went to his dresser and pulled out a long black box. "This is for you."

Faith gasped. Inside the box lay an exquisite necklace of princess cut canary diamonds with matching drop earrings. She looked up at Ryan's pleased face.

Surely he didn't mean this jewelry for her. It was worth a fortune. There must have been over fifty sparkling diamonds adorning the front of the necklace, strung on an elegant gold chain.

"You want me to wear these tonight?" They matched her dress perfectly.

"Of course."

She peered down at the necklace and back at Ryan, shaking her head.

His brows furrowed. "They're a gift, Faith. For you."

"Why?"

"Because you're my wife. And because I wanted to give you a gift."

His eyes were a raging bonfire, ever darkening smoke swirling through and mesmerizing her like a hypnotist.

"Turn around and I'll put the necklace on you."

As he leaned forward to drape the necklace over her and closed the clasp, his chest brushed against her back. His hands warmed her skin, lightly caressing the side of her throat with his thumbs.

It was impossible to concentrate when he touched her like that. She waited for him to step away, but he didn't. Instead she felt the press of his lips against the side of her neck, evoking desire so fierce she panicked. She quickly moved away and turned, escaping that fire only to see it still reflected in his smoky eyes.

"The necklace is lovely, Ryan. Thank you."

He gave her a knowing smile and nodded. "You're welcome. Put the earrings on. We'd better leave so we're not late."

"Paul and Jenelle Worthington are a prominent Las Vegas couple, frequently occupying the cover page of *Las Vegas Style* magazine," Ryan explained on the way to the restaurant. "They're both from old money."

"Old money?"

"Yeah. Paul's family has been building hotels and casinos in the Las Vegas area for almost as long as hotels have been around."

"So, why the dinner tonight?"

He shifted the Ferrari's gears. "Paul's looking to retire. The Worthingtons have no heirs to take over for them, so he wants to sell ownership in some of his hotels in order to make his business more manageable."

"And McKay Corporation wants some of those hotels."

Ryan smiled. "You got it."

Faith tried not to fidget as they approached the restaurant. She had frequently accompanied Ryan to business events. But this was business mixed with her first social appearance as his wife. She didn't want to screw this up.

"What's wrong?" Ryan asked as he whipped the vehicle around a corner.

The restaurant was only a few miles ahead. Faith inhaled deeply, trying to quell the flutters in her stomach. This was one of those times she wished Ryan didn't drive so fast. She managed a smile. "Nothing."

"You're not nervous, are you?"

She kept her eyes glued to the road, watching every sign, every landmark pass at breakneck speed.

"Me? Nervous? Of course not. What would I have to be nervous about? It's just dinner, right? Just the Worthingtons. I know how important this dinner is, and I'll try my best to do everything right. I mean, the Worthingtons have several hotels and if you bought them it could be quite a boon to McKay Corporation. I should probably have done some research on them before we left the office, then maybe—"

"Faith," Ryan interrupted.

She looked at him and drew a hasty breath. "Yes?"

"You're blabbering."

"I am?"

"Yeah, you are. Relax." He placed his hand on her knee, squeezing it gently.

Right, like *that* was going to calm her down. As if her heartbeat wasn't already racing, the heat emanating from his hand burned into the bare skin of her leg.

Then it got worse. His fingers trailed lightly above her knee. She wondered if Ryan kept any paper bags in the car. She felt an anxiety attack coming on and knew she'd be hyperventilating soon. Or maybe she'd just throw up.

"Calm down. There's nothing to be nervous about."

Easy for him to say. He did this social stuff all the time. Social for Faith was the weekly trek to the grocery store and a chat with the produce manager over the price of tomatoes. Those trips didn't entail having witty conversation.

"I'm not nervous."

He smiled. "Yes, you are. And stop it. It's just dinner."

Markham's Restaurant was an up-and-coming establishment, luring the elite clientele with the hiring of one of New York City's premier chefs. Getting a reservation less than a month in advance was next to impossible. Unless you were Ryan McKay.

The valet opened their doors, then drove away to park the car. Ryan placed his hand on the small of her back and led her inside. The intimacy of that possessive touch wasn't lost on her.

The restaurant was dark, a place for intimate conversation without fear of being overheard. Ryan stepped up to the hostess, who smiled in recognition.

"Mr. McKay," the young woman said in a honey-like voice that matched her long hair. "So nice to see you again."

Ryan nodded. "Michelle. Is our table ready?"

"Of course." Michelle grabbed two menus and led them to a booth in the back of the room. Tuxedo-clad waiters silently scurried about, unobtrusive but always available.

"The Worthingtons will be joining us shortly," he said to Michelle, who informed Ryan she'd bring them to the table as soon as they arrived.

No sooner had they sat down than their waiter arrived and Ryan ordered a bottle of wine.

Faith rubbed her fingertips against the white linen tablecloth. A vase of roses centered the table, along with two deep red tapered candles. She'd never been to Markham's before. The restaurant was dark and intimate—a perfect place for lovers to sit alone in the shadows. She took a sip of water from a crystal glass, her throat gone completely dry.

The waiter soon returned with a bottle of white wine, something French that Faith had never heard of. She sipped the smooth, dry chardonnay.

"Do you like the jewelry?" Ryan asked.

Honestly, she'd forgotten all about it. She wasn't really a jewelry person, in fact rarely wore it. "Yes, it's lovely. Thank you, again."

"It looks good against your skin." His eyes dwelled on her chest. Faith squirmed.

"Thank you." She wished he wouldn't look at her like that. His intense eyes darkened whenever they roamed over her body. "I don't usually wear jewelry."

He quirked a brow. "Really? I thought diamonds were a girl's best friend."

That made her smile. "Not this girl's. I'm not one to adorn myself with jewels. One, because of the cost, and two, it just seems, I don't know, superfluous somehow."

He looked toward the front of the restaurant and didn't say another word. But he seemed disappointed.

Before she could ask what she had said wrong, Paul and Jenelle Worthington were escorted to the table. Ryan stood, shook Paul's hand and planted a light peck on Jenelle's cheek.

"Paul, Jenelle, this is my wife, Faith."

Faith stood to greet Ryan's guests, pasting on her biggest and hopefully most professional smile. "I'm pleased to meet both of you," she said and held out her hand.

Paul shook her hand. A robust man, he looked more like a professional wrestler than a successful hotelier. Big and burly with a thick neck, he had silvery hair swept back in waves and an extremely tan complexion owing obviously to hours spent in Nevada's year-round sun.

Jenelle was tall and lithe, impeccably dressed and adorned in diamonds. Her shimmery blonde hair was bobbed and swept behind her ears, and nary a wrinkle showed on her face.

Whether that was due to plastic surgery or great genetics Faith couldn't tell.

"Darling, it's so nice to meet you," Jenelle said to Faith. She tapped Ryan's hand. "How long has this been going on, and why didn't we know about it?"

Ryan smiled. "We kept it a secret."

"Obviously," Jenelle said, her gaze flitting between Ryan and Faith as if she were looking for hidden messages. "And you were Ryan's...uhh...secretary?"

The raised eyebrows and patronizing look told Faith in an instant what Jenelle thought of her. "His executive assistant. And I still am," she replied.

"You mean you're still working?" Jenelle's hand flew to her throat in horror.

Faith tried not to smile. "Yes, I am."

"Quit badgering the girl, Jen," Paul admonished. The waiter brought him a double scotch, which he promptly downed in one gulp and asked for another.

"I'm not badgering her at all, dear." Jenelle shot her husband a scathing glare before turning her inquisitive brown eyes back to Faith. "I'm merely getting acquainted with Ryan's lovely new wife."

Faith drew back as Jenelle leaned into her, so close their noses practically touched.

"Tell me, dear," Jenelle whispered. "Did that bad boy Ryan marry you because he got you pregnant?"

It was going to be a long evening. Faith took a deep breath and prepared for the inquisition.

On the way home, Faith mentally replayed the events of the evening. She hoped she'd said and done all the right things.

Ryan and Paul had immersed themselves in business through dinner, while Faith endured Jenelle's barrage of questions about her life, her past, her education and social ambitions.

Social ambitions? She had none. When she couldn't come up with a list of social obligations, Jenelle had been horrified.

Was she supposed to volunteer for some committee? Join the Bridge Club? What? She made a mental note to ask Ryan about it later.

When they arrived home, Faith went upstairs to prepare for bed and Ryan marched into his office without a word to her.

Had she done something to upset him? At the beginning of the evening, when he gave her the jewelry, she could have sworn she read desire in his eyes.

Obviously she'd been wrong. Like she'd know what desire in a man's eyes looked like. She was certainly no expert there.

So why had he been so quiet on the way home? She'd been nice to the Worthingtons and hadn't done or said anything that should have embarrassed him.

Maybe men got moody too, just like women.

Faith hung her dress in the closet and slipped on her nightgown. She slid into bed and turned off the light.

The bed seemed overly large without Ryan in it, despite the fact she continued to keep her distance from him. She wasn't ready yet to make that intimate leap with her new husband.

But, still, the bed was too large for her to sleep in alone. Funny how quickly one's perspective could change.

Faith needed her husband in bed with her.

Ryan sat at his desk, pondering where his mission had gone wrong.

He'd bought her jewelry. Women loved jewelry. They gushed, they ooohed, they aaahed, then they jumped gratefully into bed with you.

So, why hadn't Faith?

Damn, she had looked incredible tonight. The dress clung to her curves, accentuating a body he was dying to get his hands on, and wasn't allowed to touch. Yet. He made a last ditch attempt to will the lustful feelings away.

They wouldn't leave. And despite his carefully planned round one, he was downstairs in his office, and she was upstairs in their bed.

The bed where obviously no lovemaking would occur tonight.

The diamond idea had been a complete bust. Faith acted as if he'd purchased them on some television shopping network for twenty dollars. Nothing. A polite thank you and that was it.

Why hadn't he noticed that the only jewelry she wore was her wedding ring?

Faith wasn't like other women. Obviously.

He stood and paced the dark-paneled office, skirting the oversized desk and plopping down on the plump sofa. He propped his feet on the glass coffee table, leaned back and laced his fingers together behind his neck.

Jewelry didn't do it for her. Fine, then. He had other ideas. Which strategy to employ next?

He glanced at the calendar on the wall and thought a moment. Yes, this would be a good time. Things were going well at work. Nothing pressing coming up. He could afford to take a few days off.

He loosened his tie, went back to his desk and pulled out his scheduler.

A few telephone calls and round two would be in action.

This one would work. This one would get Faith into his bed, only there wouldn't be any sleeping.

With a satisfied grin, he picked up the telephone.

Chapter Eight

Faith couldn't believe she was actually on a plane heading to Hawaii. And not a commercial airline either, but the McKay corporate jet.

Ryan was full of surprises. He'd shocked her early this morning when he announced they were going to take a few days off and go to Hawaii.

At first she thought he'd been joking, but he hadn't been. With a stern look and a glance at his watch, Ryan had informed her she had approximately one hour to throw a few things in a suitcase and get ready to leave.

Why he decided on this trip, she didn't know. But, she had to go along, as did both James and Stan.

James arrived downstairs in a less than jovial mood. They left at a little past seven in the morning, and James usually didn't rise until well after noon. But then again, Ryan told her, James always stayed out partying until almost dawn. No wonder he was tired.

Stan looked wide-eyed and ready to go, apparently more than happy to take the trip to Hawaii. That didn't surprise her, since he worked only for the McKays and could conduct his business from anywhere.

Now the four of them were shortly to land on the island of Oahu. Stan worked on his laptop, James was asleep and snoring loudly and Ryan was on the phone.

Faith gawked out the window, amazed at the expanse of ocean below her. She'd never been to Hawaii, although she'd always dreamed of it. She'd expressed her delight about the trip to Ryan, who'd only smiled enigmatically as he packed his things.

When she'd asked him if the trip was business or pleasure, his only comment was, "Pleasure, I hope. And lots of it." He'd said it with a huge grin like he'd just eaten the best dessert of his life.

Men were so strange.

The pilot announced it was time to land. Faith watched the descent of the plane into the islands with the excitement of a child, anxious to get out and explore.

The islands looked so small, she thought as they circled in preparation for landing. It was hard to believe that these tiny little islands held such attraction for so many mainlanders. But then again, her own heart pumped in anticipation of setting foot in the tropics.

The plane touched down and Faith, Ryan and their two chaperones disembarked and piled into the awaiting limo.

Their hotel, owned by the McKays, was an opulent twin-towered high rise located on Waikiki Beach. When they exited the limo, Faith didn't know where to turn her eyes first. She inhaled, filling her lungs with the heady fragrance of the abundant ginger permeating the front entryway of the hotel.

They were shown to their rooms immediately by the bellman. Faith and Ryan's top floor suite overlooked the ocean. It took up the entire floor, obviously the best one in the hotel.

"Shouldn't this suite be saved for one of the paying guests?" she asked as she followed Ryan onto the balcony.

"No. This is my personal apartment. It's never rented out to paying guests. There's another suite like it in the adjacent tower."

Personal apartment? It was more like a mansion, and bigger than most homes. The long hallway stretched as far as she could see, and Faith counted at least four bedrooms in addition to the oversized master, which had its own private balcony overlooking the ocean.

She loved the tropical decor, with wicker chairs and sofas, lazily turning ceiling fans and fresh flowers in every room. Floral pillows with hibiscus and birds of paradise decorated the well-cushioned furniture.

Right now she was transfixed on the sparkling blue ocean. Never had she seen such beauty. She could already imagine drifting off to sleep with the sounds of ocean waves lapping against the shore right outside her bedroom window.

It was almost too perfect, too inspiring. "It's beautiful."

"Yes, it is." He pulled her against his chest and wrapped his arms around her.

Despite the incessant thrumming of her heart, she rested against him, the rhythmic ocean waves calming her. The floral scents intoxicated her and Ryan's strong body made her feel more secure than she'd ever felt before. It was perfect and she never wanted to move again.

"Tell me again what we're doing here?" she asked.

"We've been working hard on the Worthington purchase. Things are flowing well at work right now, and I never got a chance to take you on a honeymoon."

Honeymoon. The one he was going to take with Erica. The one Faith thought she'd never have. She smiled.

"What would you like to do first?" he asked.

His voice sent shivers down her spine, thrilling her senses.

"I have no idea. You've been here before, what do you usually do?" She leaned her head back to see him.

He smiled and shrugged. "Nothing, really. I'm usually here on business or entertaining clients, so I'll usually have a boat or event chartered."

She pursed her lips. "That doesn't sound like fun. What if we get out and explore the island?"

She almost laughed at the look of horror on his face. Obviously he was not accustomed to mingling with the tourist population.

"Come on," she urged. "It'll be fun."

"If you say so."

Faith changed into khaki shorts and a white tank top. She slipped on her sandals and brought along a pair of tennis shoes. By the time she came out, Ryan was already waiting for her, having donned a pair of shorts and a polo shirt. She stopped and grinned at him.

"What's so funny?"

"Look at us. We're the typical tourists, even wearing the same colors."

Ryan looked at his khaki shorts and white polo shirt, then at Faith. "Great minds think alike?"

She laughed. "I guess so. Shall we?"

He had arranged for a rental car after Faith objected to touring the island in a limo, claiming she just wanted to be a tourist. Ryan didn't understand why they couldn't be tourists from a limo, but she said half the adventure was grabbing a map, driving yourself and seeing where the road takes you.

"So you're an experienced navigator?" he asked as he made his way onto the main road.

"Are you kidding? I can barely find my way around Las Vegas and I've lived there for years."

"Great. We'll be lost for sure."

"From what I see on the map," she said, scanning the cumbersome paper on her lap, "we take this road and drive around in a circle. It would be difficult to get lost."

"I hope you're right."

They spent the next few hours driving the circumference of the island. Faith stopped him several times in order to view a particular expanse of ocean, or watch surfers ride the waves, or because a certain shop caught her eye and she wanted to get out and browse.

While she shopped, he waited. And, she had to be friendly with everyone she met, so Ryan found himself waiting, while she engaged in conversation with most of the storekeepers.

Not once did she ask Ryan to buy anything for her. He found that so odd. Of course many of the things they looked at were junk, but to Faith it seemed like a treasure hunt, every shop more unique than the last, each holding items she claimed to have never seen before.

They passed several high class malls and shopping centers, but Faith didn't give them a second glance. She seemed content to browse and look.

What an unusual woman.

And all the while he couldn't take his eyes off her.

They pulled over to watch windsurfers sail their boards high into the air, only to crash back down and expertly cut through the water. Faith grabbed his hand and dragged him to the beach.

While she focused on the windsurfers, he focused on her.

Her ocean-like eyes widened with pleasure as she planted her feet in the sand near the water's edge. Oblivious to the wind whipping her hair or the salt spray on her clothes, she turned her face up and let the elements wash over her, and then laughed out loud when a crashing wave knocked her down, soaking her.

Ryan reached down to help her up and she giggled and pulled him into the water. He spit out a mouthful of salty seawater and she laughed at him.

He gazed down at her, lying like a mermaid in the water and sand. Her hair was tangled and her clothes soaked.

Desire hit him with such force it threatened to knock him back on his heels. Never before had he felt this stabbing pain, this ferocious aching need. He hardened instantly despite the uncomfortable and less than private surroundings.

Faith must have felt it too, because the smile died on her face and her eyes darkened like the sky at dusk. She didn't move to get up or away from him, despite the fact he was lying on top of her.

Ryan took her lack of objection as invitation and bent his head to the mouth he'd been dying to kiss for weeks.

Faith couldn't have objected if she wanted to. This was simply too glorious a moment, one she'd remember as long as she lived. Ryan's eyes went from light gray to smoky dark, the orbs gathering in a storm of passion so violent it shook her. She couldn't move a muscle, mesmerized by the hot desire etched on his face.

Oh God, he was going to kiss her. But instead of finding a way to avoid it, she went stock still as if any movement on her part would make him stop. She didn't want him to stop. She wanted this kiss more than she'd ever wanted anything in her life.

He cupped her cheeks with the palms of his hands and drew her toward him. His lips claimed hers and rocked her senses to a fevered pitch despite the water swirling over them. He tasted like the salty air, wild and whirling around her like a hurricane. Her body was awash in passion, flaming every nerve ending like a raging, out of control fire.

Nothing else mattered at that moment. All she knew was this man and an unprecedented need to have him touch her, kiss her, taste her.

She let him control the passionate assault on her mouth, unable to do anything but hold on for dear life. He threaded his hands into her hair, pulling her closer. But closer wasn't enough. She wanted so much more. She could have wept from the sheer pleasure of his kiss, but still she wanted more. For the first time in her life, Faith wanted. And what she wanted was Ryan.

Wanted him with an all-consuming desire that was terribly inappropriate considering their surroundings. Ryan buried his hands in her wet hair and positioned his body over her.

The sudden realization hit her like a tidal wave. What must they look like on a public beach?

She grasped his shoulders to gently push him away. He pulled back, shocking her with the smoldering intensity of his gaze.

"What's wrong?" he rasped. His husky, passion-filled voice threatened to send her back where they'd been, but common sense told her this was not the time or place.

If they continued, she knew he wouldn't stop. And she didn't have enough strength left to resist. She wanted this as much as he did.

"We're in public, Ryan. Please, let me up."

He frowned, then nodded and stood, grasping Faith's hands to pull her up.

"We'd better get back to the hotel and get this sand and salt water off," he said.

Faith couldn't help the emptiness she felt at losing that intimate contact they had briefly shared. "I suppose we should."

On the ride back she could gather no clues to how he felt. Neither happy nor angry, his expression lacked any emotion. She sighed, knowing somehow she had screwed up what was, to her, the most intensely erotic moment of her life.

They showered and prepared for dinner. Stan and James made an appearance to check on them, but both announced they had other plans and would be gone for the remainder of the evening.

Faith was pleased they wouldn't have chaperones for their first dinner together in Hawaii. This was a special night.

Ryan wanted to have a meal brought to their room, or close the restaurant downstairs so they could eat quietly and alone, but Faith had a different idea. Armed with brochures she had picked up on the way into the hotel, she was firm in her resolve to choose where they'd eat dinner. And she wanted it to be a surprise.

Ryan didn't look pleased, but said the trip was for her and she could choose any damn place she wanted to eat dinner.

Boy, was he cranky!

After their kiss that afternoon he had gone mute and took every opportunity to avoid standing anywhere in close proximity to her.

Faith had no earthly idea what she had done wrong this time. It had to be because she'd stopped their kiss.

If it had been any other location but the middle of a public beach, she would have welcomed the opportunity to continue their passionate kiss, and possibly what might have followed. Feelings and sensations she'd never known existed were suddenly available to her, and all she had to do was reach out and take them.

Little by little, the idea of making love with her husband became more appealing. Not that the thought hadn't been appealing before. How it would change her life and her relationship with Ryan had frightened her. That alone made it scary, but in a different way.

Despite her intent to remain detached, she'd jumped into the deep end and become emotionally tied to Ryan. His involvement was purely sexual. Business, of course.

It didn't matter. She knew what she was required to do in this marriage, and however she felt about it, at some point she'd have to fulfill her obligations.

But not right now. Now she had a surprise for Ryan. A surprise that hopefully would put the smile back on his face.

Ryan grumbled under his breath. She'd made him wear this awful Hawaiian shirt. He'd come out of the bedroom dressed in Dockers and a short-sleeved shirt, and there she stood in a bright blue sundress with wide white flowers plastered all over it, a gardenia in her hair and sandals on her feet.

She should have looked ridiculous, but she didn't. Damn if he didn't find her desirable in that getup. She looked like one of the island girls, with her creamy tan and sunburned nose.

Then she presented him with a shirt she'd bought him. A red shirt. With big, tropical birds on it.

Good lord!

She insisted he put it on and change into shorts, then explained it had to do with their dinner this evening and he had to be dressed appropriately.

This was appropriate? Where the hell were they going—a *Worst Dressed Tourist* contest? Faith would probably think *that* was fun. He wanted to hide his face as they headed outside the hotel. Instead, he slipped on his sunglasses and tried to blend in with the other tourists. Not too difficult considering how he was dressed.

Faith grinned. "All you need is a straw hat and you'll be set."

He threw a frown at her. "Don't even think about it."

She laughed. "All right. Shall we go?"

At least this time she'd agreed to the limo. Faith squirmed in her seat the entire ride, even giggled a few times. He swore he was traveling with an excitable child, not a grown woman.

She'd even bought one of those cheap travel cameras. He would have bought her a Nikon or Minolta if she'd asked for one. But then again she never asked him for anything.

The limo pulled to a halt in front of Oahu's Bird of Paradise Luau.

Not a luau! He stifled a groan as they exited the limo and joined the massive crowds awaiting entry outside the gate.

Faith handed him the tickets she'd purchased from the hotel concierge. And she was still grinning.

"Surprised?"

"Uh, yeah, you could say that."

"I'm so excited, Ryan. My first luau. I know this is probably old hat to you, but it's something I've always wanted to do."

He shrugged. "I've never been to one either."

Her eyes widened in shock. "Never? Really?"

"Really." He'd been lucky so far. All his trips to Hawaii and he'd never once had to deal with this overly commercialized hokey. Guess his luck had run out.

"Then it's a first for both of us!" She grabbed his hand and hurried through the gate.

Ryan trudged along beside her, desperately looking for a way out of this dilemma, but finally resigning himself to the fact he was going to have to endure the next several hours without complaint.

After all, this trip was for Faith. He wanted to show her a good time, and hopefully, just hopefully, out of sheer gratitude she'd award him with her virginity. If it took a luau to get it, he'd endure it. His goal was to make love with his wife.

To get her pregnant, of course. That's all. To meet the terms of the will. Nothing more. Just business.

Then, why did it somehow seem to be getting personal?

Maybe it was the kiss today. Had they been anywhere but on the beach, Ryan would have slipped her clothes off and made love to her right then and there. Judging from her reaction to the kiss, he didn't think she would have objected. No, he knew for certain she wouldn't have objected. Her body had melted against his, and the sounds she made told him she wanted the same thing he did.

Never before had he been so incredibly excited by a woman. He was confusing sexual desire with emotional attachment, that's all. He never got emotionally involved.

But what he'd felt with Faith today *had* been different. When her lips met his he was stunned by an all powerful, knock your socks off hit to his nether regions like he'd never experienced before. He'd gotten so hot so quick he'd forgotten all about where they were. In fact, he could have cared less had they stripped down and done the deed right there on the beach, bystanders be damned.

But it wouldn't have been right. Not for Faith—not for her first time.

Faith strolled over to the fire pit where the pig was roasting. She searched for him, then smiled and waved when she caught his eye. She wore that cheap camera around her neck like a prize, taking pictures of him, the pig, the other tourists, even the cook. Her cheeks were flushed from the heat, her blue eyes startling in their intensity. She'd never looked happier.

Or more beautiful. Or more desirable.

Ryan was glad for the long, if hideous shirt as he felt the familiar stirrings in his jeans. Not once since this afternoon had he had a coherent thought. Visions of the two of them rolling around in the ocean kept sailing across his mind.

He still wanted her. More now than ever.

"Ryan, hurry!" Faith ran over and tugged at his hand, excitedly pulling him along. "Dave and Terey have agreed to take our picture, and then we'll take theirs."

Oh great. Now she'd made friends with another couple.

Dave and Terey, it turned out, were from Minnesota and celebrating their fifteenth wedding anniversary with a trip to Hawaii.

"Now put your arm around me and smile for heaven sakes. You look like you're in pain," Faith instructed, then slipped her arm around Ryan's waist and smiled.

He did his best to give as genuine a smile as he could muster considering the circumstances, but was certain it came out looking more like he had an ulcer.

To make matters worse, after the exchange of picture-taking Faith invited Dave and Terey to sit with them during dinner.

Terey was an enthusiastic woman who liked to talk. A lot. And she was as loud as the oversized, flowered muumuu she wore.

Her husband dressed in typical tourist fashion. Dave's pink multi-flowered shirt was even more hideous than Ryan's, and blended nicely with his blinding white shorts, black socks and sandals. Topped off by the straw hat.

Ryan needed a drink.

"How long have you two been married?" Terey asked.

"A little over one month," Faith answered, glancing at Ryan with a shy smile.

"Newlyweds!" Terey exclaimed loud enough for the other five hundred people to hear. "How wonderful! Is this your honeymoon, then?"

"Um..."

"Yes it is," Ryan answered at Faith's hesitation. "Unfortunately, I had some pressing business matters come up right after the wedding, so our honeymoon had to be delayed."

Faith shot him a grateful smile and slipped her hand in his. His body responded to her casual touch with a shot right to his groin. His heartbeat skyrocketed when he inhaled and caught a whiff of her scent as she leaned toward him. She smelled like gardenias and ocean, stimulating and sensual and making him squirm. He took the advantage and pressed a light kiss against her lips. God, she tasted sweet. Like a ripe peach about to burst. She smiled and didn't try to move away. A very good sign.

Ryan forced his thoughts away from mentally undressing his wife to more non-sexual areas, like McKay Corporation's financial statements.

They sipped ridiculous drink concoctions that tasted like they had more fruit than alcohol. They even came with paper umbrellas that Ryan flung on the floor before downing his drink in one large gulp. Then he ordered another. And another.

After a long and agonizing wait, dinner was ready. They were herded off to stand in yet another line, trays in hand and looking at more food than a platoon of soldiers could eat in a month. Judging from the mounds on some of the guests' plates, many were going to eat their month's worth tonight.

Faith placed small samples of several things on her tray. All the while, she and Terey talked and laughed as if they'd known each other for years.

Ryan wished Faith wasn't being so friendly and outgoing. And he got stuck listening to Dave banter on and on about the chances of the Minnesota Twins in the next World Series, and how he had personally met one the team's formerly prominent short-stops in the men's room in the box seat section one game. Obviously the high point of Dave's life.

Downing another mystery drink, Ryan prayed for rain.

The sky was clear and almost every star was visible.

It figured.

When dinner was over, Ryan stood to leave but Faith grabbed his arm and pulled him down.

"Where are you going? The entertainment's about to begin."

Ryan rolled his eyes to the celestial heavens and ordered another drink.

By the time they'd sat through the hula dancers, fire breathers, spouting volcano and twenty different Hawaiian songs, Ryan was done for. Oh, man, was he ever done for. Maybe it was the ten or so Mai Tais he'd drank, hoping for oblivion. Unfortunately, it hadn't worked. He was still conscious.

Faith had seemed to enjoy herself. She'd caught his eye several times during the show, smiling with a hopeful expression on her face. He tried his best to appear enthusiastic, although getting blitzed wasn't helping the situation.

At least the show was over. They said their goodbyes to Terey and Dave. But not before Faith had exchanged telephone numbers and vowed the four of them would get together again soon. Ryan held his tongue and smiled a polite goodbye, nodding when the couple said they'd see him on their next trip because they planned to come to Las Vegas.

Terey and Dave. In Las Vegas. Visiting him?

Not in this lifetime.

He weaved his way to the limo. Faith, on the other hand, seemed to be stone-cold sober. He swore she'd drank at least half as much as he did. Surely she should be feeling something. Maybe she'd loosened up enough that she'd go for a romp in the hay.

He snickered. Perhaps his plan was working after all.

"What's so funny?" she asked as they entered their hotel room.

Ryan crashed his left shoulder into the doorway as he walked through. "Nothin'."

She squinted, well, actually both of her did.

"Ryan, are you all right?"

Why were there two sofas in this room when there had only been one before they'd left earlier? He opened his eyes wider to focus, hoping when he sat down it really was a couch and not the floor.

"I'm fine. Why?" Oh good. It *was* a couch.

The room began to spin. Interesting, and kind of nauseating, too.

"I think those cocktails were a bit strong tonight, don't you?" she asked.

Great. She was hammered, too. Time for beddy-bye. He wondered where their bedroom was. Probably too far away. They'd have to do it on the couch because he was certain he wasn't going to be able to get up.

"Come over here and sit down by me, here on the sofa, yeah, right here." He patted the soft cushion next to him. And yawned.

Faith strolled over and sat. "Are you sure you're all right?"

Why wasn't she drunk? "Why aren't you drunk?"

She shrugged and grinned at him. "I don't get drunk. For some reason I metabolize alcohol quite well."

He waved his hand in the air. "Me too. I mabolize calohol kite well too." He wondered if she was aware that she now had two heads.

"I think we should get you in bed."

"Now yer talkin', babe. Let's go get it on." He attempted to rise but fell back onto the couch. He wrinkled his nose, looked at Faith and then shrugged. "Okay I can't gedup. Les jus do it right here."

Uh oh. She was fading away, lost in the tornadic spinning of the room. He tried to raise his hand to wave goodbye to her, but everything went dark.

❦

He was dead. Quite obviously, someone had murdered him in his sleep. With a sledgehammer to the head, judging from the excruciating pain shooting from one ear to the other.

Oh God, he'd gone to heaven! Blinding light shot into his eyes, causing the pain to migrate from between his ears to the back of his head. He felt miserable. Dead, miserable, and blinded by the light.

Correction. He was in hell. That had to be it. Heaven would never be this painful.

"Good morning."

No, it was heaven, he decided. He'd just heard an angel's voice whispering softly in his ear.

"Good morning, angel." He smiled and mumbled into his pillow. "Is this heaven?"

"I doubt you'll think it's heaven when you're fully awake. Bet you have a miserable headache this morning."

He slowly pried open one eye and peered out.

This wasn't heaven. Although Faith did look like an angel in her white silk nightgown. Perhaps if he reached for her...

"Ugh. I feel awful!" He sat up as the sharp pain stabbed his brain.

"It's no wonder considering how much you drank last night." His merciful angel held a glass of water and two aspirin in her hand.

"Thanks." He swallowed and looked at her. "I got drunk, didn't I?"

She smiled at him. "I'll say. Passed right out on the couch."

"So how did I end up in here?"

She placed the glass on the nightstand, then folded her hands in front of her, a pink blush on her face. "I coaxed you in with the promise of sex. You at least had the desire to make it this far before collapsing on the middle of the bed."

He tilted his head as the thought struck him. "And did we?"

"Did we what?"

"Have sex."

Her lips curled upward. "No." Her voice was almost a whisper. Ryan found her shyness endearing. But, damn. No sex.

"And would you have? If I had been able to?"

Her clear blue eyes focused on his. "Honestly? I don't know."

Chapter Nine

Would she have made love with Ryan that night? Faith didn't have an answer. The thought occupied her mind on the plane trip back to Las Vegas.

Maybe if he'd been sober she'd have considered it. After the kiss they'd shared the day of the luau, she knew without a doubt she'd have fallen easily into bed with Ryan that night.

But the fates conspired against them, and maybe that was a sign that the time wasn't yet right.

They'd had three wonderful days in Hawaii, soaking up the sun, playing tourist and enjoying the wondrous sights and smells. It had been relaxing, calming, and above all, had given her time to think about Ryan.

Without a doubt, she was attracted to her husband. He'd awakened needs she hadn't realized she possessed. The need to be wanted and desired.

He'd been good to her—very good to her—since they married. Caring, considerate and fun. Not at all what she had expected. And they *would* eventually have to make love. It was ridiculous to put it off any longer, so why was she?

After the luau Ryan had been incapable. But why not tonight? Or any night after? What held her back?

She'd had a great time. And Ryan seemed to relax, although not completely. After the night he got drunk and passed out, he never brought up the subject of sex again.

And that disappointed her.

Time to put her mind elsewhere. Working at the animal shelter today should help. She'd been away for too long and missed volunteering there, cuddling the dogs and especially the kittens.

"Where's your husband this morning?" James strolled into the kitchen, dressed for a game of tennis.

"He's in his home office doing some paperwork."

"I see. And how's the marriage going?"

"Fine." She was wary of saying anything that might give James the impression that she and Ryan's relationship wasn't proceeding according to the terms of Quentin McKay's will.

"You know he's going to dump you as soon as he gets you pregnant, don't you?" James said with a smirk.

Her irritation grew as she realized what he was doing. She pushed the newspaper aside and gave him her full attention. "I know the terms of the will."

"There are a lot of things about Ryan you don't know." He pulled a chair and sat next to her. His face, so similar to Ryan's, was etched with concern. She didn't believe it for one second. Faith knew what he was after.

"I don't need to know everything about him."

"But there are things you should know. Take his almost-wife Erica, for example. I'll bet you didn't know that the two of them—"

"Hey, is there any coffee left?" Ryan strolled into the kitchen and Faith sat back in her chair, feeling guilty that she'd even taken the time to listen to James's lies in the first place.

Although she really would have liked to hear the remainder of his last sentence. Erica? Wasn't she out of the picture? Surely Ryan had no further contact with her after she'd walked out on him at the last minute—when he'd needed her the most.

Ryan grabbed a cup and leaned against the kitchen island, his gaze flitting to both her and James. Faith averted her eyes, feeling guilty that she'd been talking to Ryan's cousin.

"What were you two talking about?" Ryan asked.

James shrugged and rose from the table. "Just getting better acquainted. I'm off to play tennis. See you later."

After he left, Ryan sat in the chair James vacated. "What was that all about?"

"Uhh, nothing. I think he was fishing for information about the two of us. I'm not sure."

Ryan nodded. "Doesn't surprise me. It's in his best interest if our marriage fails. Don't let him catch you off-guard. He'll continue to pry, wanting to trip you up or say anything that will nullify our marriage. Be careful. There's a lot at stake here."

"Yes. I'm fully aware what's at stake."

"Good. I knew I could count on you."

No emotion whatsoever. To Ryan, their marriage was like another deal in the works—another negotiation, another takeover. And of course, he planned to win.

Faith stood and put her cup in the dishwasher, then turned around. "I'll be gone most of the day today."

"Where to?" He grinned. "Shopping?"

"Perish the thought." She offered a shudder for emphasis. Her closet overflowed from their first shopping expedition. It was doubtful she'd ever need to shop again. Except for maternity clothes. The thought brought a smile.

Of course, to get pregnant, she'd have to have sex.

135

Soon.

"And here I thought you liked shopping."

"No, I'm going to the animal shelter."

"What for?"

"I volunteer there on weekends. I haven't gone in the past few weeks because of everything else going on. I really need to go."

"Animal lover, are you?" He leaned back in the chair, his jeans-clad legs spread out. His black V-neck sweater hugged his chest in ways that made heat pool deep inside her.

She sighed. What a fine male specimen he was. If only...no, she wouldn't think about it right now. "I've got to get going. They're expecting me at ten."

"Have fun, then," he said and picked up the newspaper she'd discarded, already dismissing her from his thoughts.

Ryan watched her leave, then set the newspaper down. Animal shelter? That was a side of her he knew nothing about.

And what about the guilty look on her face? When he'd walked in and found her in the kitchen with James, she'd been hanging on his cousin's every word like the man was the most gifted of storytellers.

Yeah, right. James had barely slipped through high school and had his college degree purchased for him with McKay endowments. He definitely wasn't gifted. So what had James said to Faith that captured her interest? She hadn't seemed to want to tell him about it.

His wife was an enigma. Purity and naiveté that he'd never seen in a woman her age. But also shrouded in mystery. There were so many things about her he didn't know.

And she was apparently completely immune to him. Not once had he received any signals from her that she was ready or willing to make love with him. Except for that kiss on the beach. Even that she had stopped. And right when things were getting interesting, too.

He'd done everything in his power to convince her. He'd bought her a new wardrobe, encouraged her to change her hairstyle and wear makeup. Hell, she'd even stopped wearing those goofy owl glasses she really didn't need.

Then he'd bought her jewelry, and taken her to Hawaii.

But had he been rewarded with the gift of her virginity in return?

No.

Although she had intimated that if he hadn't been drunk the night of the luau, something might have happened. But, would it have, really? Doubtful.

What was it going to take to seduce that woman? An Act of Congress?

He was fresh out of ideas.

And the clock was ticking.

CB

Faith wiped her nose with the tissue she'd dug out of her purse, hoping the tears would dry up by the time she walked in the house.

She sniffed, wanting nothing more than to sit on the front porch stoop and bawl like a baby. Really, she'd been doing this for years. One would think she'd be hardened to it by now.

But she wasn't. Every time it happened it broke her heart, tore her up, and took her days to get over it.

If Ryan saw her like this, knew the reasons behind it, he'd think her a child. She was a grown up, and needed to be more stoic.

She dropped her purse on the porch and sat on one of the wicker chairs, focusing on the view as a hopeful distraction. The view of the Las Vegas strip was breathtaking. The McKay mansion sat atop a hill overlooking the best sight in town.

The lights weren't as visible now as they would be in the dark, but the sun had begun its slow descent over the horizon, lighting up the glitzy hotels lining gambling central. And right in the middle of all the grandeur sat The Chalet, its stark white towers looming like Heaven's gate in the middle of Babylon.

She swiped at the tears continuing their relentless roll down her cheeks, willing herself to stop crying. She really needed to learn to hold her emotions in.

"Mrs. McKay, is something wrong?"

Faith turned to see Leland standing at the front door, ever formal as usual. She hadn't even heard him open the door.

"No," she sniffed. "I'm fine."

He stepped outside and pulled the front door partly shut. "You're crying."

"Just a little."

"Is there something I can do?"

"It's silly, really."

Leland pulled a chair and sat next to her. Funny, he never sat when she did.

"Would you like to tell me about it?" he asked.

She smiled at him, touched that he would even consider asking. "I volunteer at the animal shelter."

He nodded.

"Someone brought a litter of kittens in, along with the mother cat today."

"Go on."

She sniffed again. "The vet checked them and they all had feline leukemia, were malnourished and had to be put down."

"I see."

The tears fell again, despite her efforts to keep them at bay. Leland handed her a handkerchief, which she accepted gladly.

"I told you it was silly." she said.

"It's not silly to you."

"They were so sweet, even the mama. But, because their owner hadn't had her tested, she passed it on to her babies. Oh, and Leland," she said as she turned and rested her hand on his knee, "they were adorable. Orange-and-white–striped, like little tigers." She couldn't hold it in any longer. She burst into tears, burying her face in Leland's handkerchief.

Leland placed his arm around her shoulders and patted, offering what to him must have been an unprecedented amount of emotion.

"Thank you," she managed when she could catch a breath. "I don't know what's gotten into me today, but every time they put one of those sweet little things to death a part of me dies too."

"You love animals."

She nodded. "I was never allowed pets as a child, and my apartment has rules against them, so I've never had one of my own. That's why I volunteer. So I can at least be around them once a week, but then when they have to be..."

There she went again. She was a basket case, pure and simple. Leland continued to pat her back. He really was so sweet to her. He and Margaret both. Over the past weeks she'd come to think of them as family. Truthfully, they were the only family she had.

Leland stayed with her in the growing darkness and held her until she'd finished crying over the lost babies.

Thank God Ryan hadn't been the one to see her out here blubbering like a baby over a few dead kittens.

CȜ

Faith hadn't seen her husband all evening. After her crying jag she'd gone to her room to wash her face. At dinner, Margaret told her Ryan had gone to the office to do a few things and would be back later in the evening.

Margaret and Leland went to a movie, so that left Faith home alone. After a relaxing shower, she spent the evening curled up on the window seat with a book.

Funny how just a few short weeks ago this was her normal routine. Now it seemed...lonely.

The front door opened and she heard Ryan's voice followed by his footsteps up the stairs. Instead of opening the door he spoke to her from outside.

"Faith? Are you in there?"

How strange. "Yes, of course. Is the door locked?" She started toward the door to check.

"Don't move!"

She halted mid-stride. "Okay. What's wrong?"

"Nothing. Turn away from the door and close your eyes."

Now what? More jewelry? Faith sighed, hoping he hadn't gotten extravagant with her again. Really, fancy jewels just weren't her style. She did as he asked and turned to face the window.

"Are you turned around?"

His voice had an excited edge to it. No matter what it was, she was going to act surprised and delighted, not wanting to disappoint him. "Yes, I'm turned around."

"Are your eyes closed?"

"Yes, Ryan, they're closed."

She waited in the middle of the bedroom, feeling a little foolish. She heard the door open and shivered when his warm breath caressed her shoulder.

"Still closed?" he whispered.

"Yes."

Nothing happened for a few seconds. She felt a tickle at her nose, and then her cheek, as something soft and fuzzy was passed against her face. She frowned, trying to imagine what in the world he had in his hands.

Then she heard the sound.

A soft mewling.

Her eyes flew open and in the palm of Ryan's hand was a tiger-striped kitten. She gasped and turned to her husband.

Ryan smiled like a man who knew he had just found the perfect gift for his wife.

"Oh my God!" she exclaimed as he handed the small kitten to her. She cradled it in her arms and ran her palm against its back, feeling its rhythmic purring. Her traitorous eyes welled with tears again, but this time they were tears of joy.

"I can't believe you did this. How did you know?"

"I eavesdropped on you and Leland outside today." He slid a loose tendril of hair behind her ear. "I'm sorry about the kittens, Faith. I know that must have been difficult for you."

He stroked her cheek so softly, his voice so sincere she was certain she was going to need more hankies soon. She picked up the kitten and held it at eye level. Its clear blue eyes stood out in contrast against its orange fur.

"This is mine? I can keep it?"

"Of course you can," he said as he stroked the kitten's head with his fingertip. "Kinda cute, isn't he?"

She sniffed, too overcome with emotion to even make an attempt at holding back. Tough businessman Ryan McKay had bought his wife a kitten. "Yes. Yes he is. I still can't believe you did this for me. Where did you get him?"

"At one of the animal shelters."

"Oh, Ryan." More tears spilled. "That's just perfect."

"I also bought a bed, litter box, food and some toys. If they're not the right kinds of things, you can take them back to the pet store and exchange them."

"I'm sure they're just fine." She shook her head, unable to believe this side of him. He touched her heart with this gesture like no jewelry or tropical vacations ever could.

They set up Tiger, as Faith named him, in the upstairs bathroom. He had plenty of tile floor to romp on and ample space for his bed, food and litter box. They sat on the floor and laughed at the kitten's antics, including its futile attempts to pull the toilet paper completely off the roll.

Despite Ryan's deep, resounding voice admonishing the kitten, Tiger was relentless. He played like a true wild thing for all of thirty minutes until he was completely worn out. His belly full, he passed out in his tiny little bed.

Ryan closed the door on the bathroom and turned to Faith.

"I think he's out for the night."

She nodded, so full of joy her heart couldn't contain it all. She regarded her husband in a new light. "Yes, I'm certain he is." She stepped toward him, stopping no more than a hand's width away. Ryan's eyes widened.

"Thank you." She pressed a light kiss to his lips.

"You're very welcome," he replied, his gray eyes darkening.

"I can't believe you did this for me."

"My pleasure."

Certain now more than ever of the life-changing step she intended to take this evening, she laid her hands upon his shoulders and inched closer, molding herself to him until their bodies touched, watching his eyes widen with surprise. "Your pleasure? I don't think so. That's about to come."

Without hesitation she slid one hand behind his neck and pulled his head down, pressing her mouth against his.

Chapter Ten

Ryan was sure he was dreaming all this. Faith's warm lips pressed gently against his, the tip of her tongue dancing lightly along the edge of his mouth.

He could tell she wasn't well practiced in the art of seduction. That excited him, knowing what she gave to him she'd never given to another man. Archaic way of thinking, but he couldn't help but feel immense satisfaction at being the first man to make love to her.

She threaded her fingers through his hair and pressed her body closer, an unspoken invitation he wasn't about to turn down.

In less than an instant he was hard and ready for her. He slid his hands around her waist, pulling her against his tortured heat.

How could innocence taste this erotic? Maybe it was the complete lack of hesitation in her kiss. She held nothing back, gave all of herself freely, abandoning herelf to the moment.

He brushed his lips over hers, searching her tongue out and finding it, tasting it, sliding his over hers in an intensely erotic interplay that left them both breathless.

"Faith, are you sure?" He pulled back and searched her face for uncertainty, but found none.

She nodded. "Yes, absolutely sure. Make love to me, Ryan."

He needed no further urging and swept her into his arms, her silk gown draping over him. He laid her on the bed and stood at the edge, watching her.

Her hair spread out like a silken, sable fan across the pillow. One lacy strap of gown slipped off her shoulder, exposing the soft, round top of her breast. She seemed completely relaxed, one arm thrown over her head and the other resting across her middle.

At that moment he wished he were an artist so he could capture the look on her face. Her eyes sparkled invitingly, as if she held all the secrets he yearned to discover.

The side slit on the gown parted, showing a slender leg. Ryan swallowed, his throat gone dry at the sight of this wanton creature spread before him.

Her hungry eyes fixed on his as he removed his shoes and pulled the sweater over his head. Her breathing quickened and his gaze focused on that small pink tongue as she licked her lips.

He couldn't get undressed fast enough.

The thought of ripping his clothes off appealed to him, but he didn't want to frighten her. Instead, he slowly slipped out of his jeans and boxers and settled on the bed next to her. He waited for a reaction, but instead of fear her expressive blue eyes gleamed in anticipation. His heart rammed in his chest in an effort to pump the blood racing through his body.

He'd never wanted a woman more than he wanted Faith. Despite his self-protestations about this being nothing more than sex, he felt connected to her. Invisible threads bound them together. The thought should have frightened him, made him wary. It didn't. It simply felt right.

She swallowed, followed by a shaky sigh.

"Are you nervous?" he whispered as he scooted closer to her.

"Not really. I've waited a long time for this moment, Ryan." She snuggled against him and trailed her fingertip up his arm, then grasped his biceps and slowly slid her hand down to his wrist.

Didn't she know what that did to him? That stroking, soft and gentle, her hands running like silk over his sensitive skin. He wanted her to touch him everywhere, just like that.

Especially in the place that was hard and throbbing.

She kept up her assault on his skin. "I know it's nothing to you, but to me it's a once in a lifetime thing. Silly, I know, but still important."

Nothing? Was she kidding? Making love to Faith was everything to him. He wanted to make this moment special for her, wanted her to know he didn't take this gift lightly, no matter what she may think.

"It's important to me too. More than you know."

Her eyes captivated him, so open and honest. "I know. This is about business, about your grandfather's will."

She seemed to accept that as fact. She thought this was all about the will?

He leaned up on his elbow and stilled her hand. "This isn't at all about business. Not tonight. Tonight it's personal. It's you and me—a man and woman together. It's about making love, and nothing else."

Her eyes glistened and he swept away the single tear that dropped down her cheek.

"What do you want me to do?" she asked.

The question made his heart crumble. He watched the play of eagerness mixed with uncertainty cross her face.

Tangling his fingers in her soft hair, he breathed in her sweet scent. "This isn't a scripted event. There are no rules. We'll take it slow—touch each other, kiss each other, and let it happen naturally."

"I'll try."

But her body tensed. If she became overly nervous it wasn't going to be pleasurable for her. And it meant everything to him that her first experience with lovemaking was one she would remember fondly, without regret.

"Sit up," he commanded with a gentle pull on her hands.

He placed her in the middle of the bed and positioned himself behind her, massaging at the tension in her shoulders. He whispered to her softly, reassuring her, telling her how beautiful she was, how desirable. Eventually she relaxed as he continued his leisurely work on the knots.

When his erection pressed against her back, she scooted towards him, rather than away. The feel of her rubbing against him was sweet torture. He wanted—needed—to be inside her, but his needs had to wait.

Right now it was more important that she relaxed. When he was certain she was calm, he leaned forward and pressed a kiss to the back of her neck. She shivered.

"That feels nice," she said.

"Good," he murmured, his lips sliding over to that luscious spot between her neck and shoulder, lightly kissing and nipping the tender flesh. He heard the sharp rise and fall of her breathing, felt her shudder.

He grasped the scraps of lace at her shoulders and pulled them down, baring her to the waist.

"Your back is beautiful," he said as his fingers slid over her spine, smiling as he felt the goose bumps rise. "Your skin is incredibly soft."

"Your hands are warm," she said, her voice growing raspier with every breath.

He moved around on the bed to face her.

And time stopped.

A pink blush covered her skin, only adding to the allure of her body. His gaze traveled over her slender collarbone, the freckles on the top of her chest, the perfection of her breasts. Her nipples puckered and she brought her hands up to cover herself. Ryan caught her hands in his.

"Don't. You're beautiful, Faith."

The look in her eyes tore him apart. Blatant desire colored their depths until they were like an azure sky at dusk. She wore every emotion in her eyes. It took all the restraint he had to keep from pressing her on the bed and plunging into her waiting heat, but he knew that would be only for him, not for her.

Tonight was for her.

With as much patience as he could muster, he lifted his hand and circled one breast, playing with the taut nipple until she gasped. Her eyes followed his fingers, seemingly mesmerized with their effect on her body.

He leaned over and lightly flicked his tongue over one peak, and she practically shot off the bed. She arched her back and moaned, long and low.

"Ryan, that feels so...wonderful."

She was killing him. She tilted her head back and exposed her neck While he grasped both breasts in his hands, alternating his mouth on each until the peaks were stiff. He removed his mouth and looked at his handiwork, supremely satisfied at the sight of her glistening nipples, moistened from his tongue and tight with desire.

He gently pressed her back on the bed and slid the gown over her hips and down her long legs.

This was the body she'd hidden all these years? This perfectly sculpted treasure? Her hips were full and made for a man's hands. He ached with the need to grasp them and pull her to him. But he fought for control, knowing if he moved too fast he'd ruin the mood.

The feel of her skin against his almost sent him over the edge. She was soft where he was hard. He wanted to drive into her, hard and fast, and release the need he'd felt for too long.

But still, he didn't.

"Tell me what you're thinking," he said, lightly stroking her breasts and belly, his fingers traveling ever lower towards the dark curls between her thighs. She was so wet, pouring over his exploring fingers.

Her eyes widened. "Wh...what?"

"I want to know what you're thinking. Right now." He didn't even recognize himself. This wasn't like him at all. His usual forays into sex consisted of heavy kissing and touching and once the lovemaking was over that was it. No talking, no murmuring, no coaxing.

But this was Faith, and she made it special.

"I'm thinking how beautiful your body is. And how..."

A blush stained her cheeks. Damn if she didn't look like one of those cherub paintings.

"Tell me. It's all right, Faith. Tell me anything you want."

She hesitated, her eyelashes fluttering against her cheek. "I've never...that is, I'd like to..." she stammered, angling her gaze to his cock.

Her innocence humbled him, made him realize what this moment meant to her. And where she was looking? Damn, it made him hot just to think of her hands on him.

This was going to require the patience of a saint. "Go ahead. Touch me."

When her palm circled his engorged flesh he arched back in pleasure. He gritted his teeth and let her explore, her hand sliding over his engorged flesh with easy motions.

"Harder," he said. "I won't break."

She squeezed, then stroked him, her gaze riveted on his cock as she moved her hand up and down his shaft. The sound of her escaping sigh tightened his desire and he knew if he didn't stop her it would be over before it started.

With a shudder he grasped her hand, removing it from his tortured flesh.

"Did I do something wrong?" she asked.

"Oh, hell no. You did everything right. So right, in fact, that I don't want to finish too fast."

"Oh."

That sweet blush stained her cheeks again. God, she was irresistible. He captured her mouth in a slow, devastating kiss that rocked his senses, then slid his mouth from her lips to her neck and back again, nipping and licking until she pushed his head toward her breasts. He complied happily, surrounding first one, then the other tight nipple. With deliberate patience he teased and rolled his tongue around each rosy crest until she cried out. Her fingers threaded through his hair, pulling him closer to her, begging without words for fulfillment.

Ryan's world changed right before his eyes. He'd never felt this way about a woman before. He wanted to possess her. And not just for tonight. The thought of any other man but him touching her, ever claiming what he was about to claim, was unimaginable.

She was his.

Faith wanted to die. She wanted to scream, rejoice and rail at him. What Ryan did to her was criminal. Need and desire she'd never felt before, never even knew existed, bound her with ropes of sensual bliss. She climbed higher and higher with every touch of his heated hands, every stroke of his tongue against her inflamed nipples. Her mind and body cried out, wanting more until she was sobbing her need. He rose up and claimed her lips once more.

His body was perfection. She only wished she had arms long enough to reach out and touch every inch of him. There would be time for exploration later. Part of her recognized that fact. But still, right now, she wanted all of him.

This was the man she'd wanted for years. Since the first day she nervously walked into his office and interviewed for the job. That day she fell in love with him.

Today she loved him even more. Tonight she'd become his wife—finally, officially, and with all the rights and pleasures she'd denied herself for so many years.

The words of her mother became no more than a distant shadow of memory. She *was* worthy of this, she deserved to feel this way. Beautiful, desired and wanted. Ryan told her, and she believed him. For the first time in her life she believed.

"You're perfect," he murmured against her throat. He trailed kisses over her breasts and belly, then moved lower, shocking her as his tongue circled her navel, and traveled even further down.

She dared to open her eyes, afraid of what she'd see and too curious not to look. Ryan's eyes hardened to a stormy silver, a devilish smile on his face as his gaze held hers and he took one long, slow taste of her.

Whether she'd just entered heaven or hell, she wasn't certain. She tilted her head back and fisted her hands in the sheets as his tongue and lips pleasured her, driving her nearly mad with sensation. It was like a fever, a madness coiling up inside her. She moaned and gasped in a near delirious state, mindless of anything except the feel of his lips on her throbbing sex. She felt her moist desire flowing over his tongue.

Through a cloud of passion his velvet voice coaxed her, encouraged her to let go, to let him possess this secret part of her. Ecstasy was within her grasp, and finally she could hold back no longer. She arched her back and screamed as the orgasm overtook her. Her body writhed against his greedy mouth, as if she could somehow escape the intensity of the gift he gave her.

He held her, stroked her until some semblance of sanity returned. Her breath came out in raspy moans as she struggled for coherent thought.

Before she could gather her composure he laid his body over hers, a satisfied glint in his smoke-filled eyes. He positioned his cock against her throbbing core, awakening it yet again as he slid slowly and delicately along its slick folds.

"I've waited an eternity to make love to you, Faith."

His words brought stinging tears to her eyes as the sincerity of them tugged at her heart. She raised her hips and wrapped her legs around him, feeling the tip of his shaft penetrate her, her moist heat welcoming him until one quick thrust later he slid inside her completely.

There was very little pain. She was beyond feeling anything but the satisfying fullness of him as he withdrew and entered her again.

Incapable of words, she clutched at him, only able to gasp her delight as tears rolled over her cheeks. She hoped he'd understand the intensity of the experience—what it meant to her. They weren't tears of sadness, but joy that such delight existed. That it could be this way between two people.

"It's heaven on earth to be inside you," he breathed in short rasps against her ear.

She threaded her fingers through his hair and pulled his head back. Their eyes met, their lips tangling together in wild abandon as he steadily increased his thrusts.

She felt that sweet tension build again as he lengthened within her, his strokes measured and quickening like his breathing, taking her with him in a wild storm of passion. He moved, and she met his thrusts with an arch of her hips. His hands swept over her fevered flesh like a reverent caress, urging the raging storm inside her. The jolt was like rapid lightning, arcing through her ever faster. When she whimpered, feeling the tempest approaching, he roared out her name as he spilled inside her. She went with him gladly, both her body and her heart forever a part of him.

She was his.

Long moments passed before Faith could breathe normally. Their sweat-soaked bodies remained joined. She didn't want to be separated from him.

For the first time in her life, she belonged to someone.

She belonged to Ryan. Maybe not forever, but for now she was his, and he belonged to her. Only her.

He swept the moist tendrils of her hair away from her face and smiled down at her. "Are you all right?"

She nodded and stroked his back. "Never better."

"Did I hurt you?"

"Not at all."

He cradled her face in his hands. "I need to ask you a question."

She nodded.

"Why now? Why tonight? What changed your mind?"

"You mean about making love?"

He nodded and smiled sheepishly. "I have to admit, I tried everything to get you in bed. Jewelry, a new wardrobe, even the trip to Hawaii. And nothing. So why now?"

She should have been angry with him, trying to buy her virginity like that, but she wasn't. On some level she understood the type of women Ryan normally associated with. He *could* buy his way into their beds. But that didn't work on her.

"It was the kitten."

His eyes widened in surprise. "The kitten? Why?"

She smiled and ran her fingertip along his jaw, loving the erotic feel of his stubble against her skin. "You brought me that kitten because I felt bad, and you wanted to make me feel better. That's what convinced me."

"The kitten?"

"Yes."

"I didn't get you the kitten to get you into bed, Faith."

"I know. But Ryan, the best gift is always the one that comes from the heart."

His eyes clouded over and he bent down, touching his forehead to hers. Then he took her lips in a tender kiss. She felt his heart in that kiss—the depth of feeling he was unable to verbalize.

"You amaze me, Faith. Every damn day you amaze me."

"Is that a good thing?"

He nodded. "A very good thing." He rolled away and trailed his finger over her stomach and hips. She shivered at the loss of his warmth against her skin.

"Are you sure I didn't hurt you?"

"On the contrary, I've never felt so good. Now I wish I hadn't insisted on waiting so long. Why didn't you tell me what I was missing?"

He rolled his eyes and grabbed her around the waist, tickling her. She squealed with laughter and grabbed for him, discovering he was extremely ticklish himself. He jumped off the bed and headed into the bathroom.

She followed behind him, admiring his magnificent rear end with a new wifely appreciation. "Well, you're the expert here. How was I supposed to know how great it was going to be?"

He turned on the shower and leaned against the bathroom counter, ogling her. She should have felt self-conscious, but didn't. He'd already seen everything anyway, had touched her in ways more intimate than anything she could have imagined. Modesty would be pointless from here on out.

"And if I had told you what you were missing, would you have believed me?"

Her lips quivered in a futile attempt to remain straight-faced. "Probably not. I didn't think you really wanted me anyway."

"Didn't want you? I've wanted you from the minute I saw you in that wedding dress, looking like a princess. As soon as I touched you, I knew I had to have you."

He grabbed her hand and pulled her into the oversized shower, turning her back to him so he could soap her. "Besides," he added as he lathered her back, "you insisted on a waiting period so you could be convinced of my incredible charm before agreeing to gift me with your virginity."

She laughed at him, half turning to stick out her tongue. "I'm still waiting to see this so-called incredible charm of yours."

He pulled her around, slid his soapy hands around her and grabbed her ass, pulling her tight against him. Her eyes widened as she felt his growing erection.

"It's right here," he said with a mischievous grin.

She threw her head back and laughed, then slid her arms around his neck, wiggling closer to his hardened length. "Charming," she replied as she opened her lips for his kiss. "Incredibly charming."

Chapter Eleven

He'd created a sex monster.

Ryan propped his exhausted head on the pillows and listened to Faith singing in the shower. The predawn light filtered through the curtains in their bedroom, promising a warm and sunny day.

He wished he could stay in bed through all of it and catch up on the sleep he'd lost the past few weeks.

The woman was insatiable, wanting him all hours of the day and night. Scandalous too, seducing him in his office in broad daylight, hundreds of staff members just down the hall.

He'd tried to resist, he really had, but finally just gave up, realizing he'd have to stand ready to appease the lust-starved dynamo he'd married.

No doubt about it, he was having the time of his life.

He grinned as he listened to her sing, cheerful as she could be. She wasn't getting much sleep either, yet didn't seem to care.

Life with Faith was full of surprises and Ryan thought he was long past surprise. He knew women well. Knew how to seduce them, what pleased them, how to let them down with kind words and token gifts so there were never any hard feelings. Yeah, he knew how to buy them off. He thought he knew everything.

Wrong. He didn't know Faith.

The fact she'd made love with him because he'd brought her the kitten touched him. But he didn't tell her that. He'd been taught quite well never to reveal his emotions to anyone. His grandfather had never been comfortable with any type of outburst or expression of feelings. Whenever Ryan had reacted emotionally to his grandfather, he'd received a lecture. Emotions made one vulnerable.

And Ryan McKay was never vulnerable.

So he enjoyed the time he spent with Faith. Which didn't mean he had feelings for her. He couldn't have feelings for her, wouldn't allow it. The last thing he needed was to fall in love with his wife. That wasn't in the plan.

"Morning, tiger," she purred as she exited the dressing area clad in a skimpy towel. She leaned over and kissed him.

He admired her legs. "Are you talking to me or the ferocious beast trying to grab your towel?"

She followed his eyes to the kitten who'd trailed a loose thread from the towel, attacking it with all the tenacity of a jungle cat. Tiger even growled—mewled was more like it, but to the kitten it was surely a fierce roar.

She laughed. "You're my big tiger, he's the little one."

"Your big tiger is exhausted. Are you trying to kill me so you can take all my money?"

She gave him a look that melted him to the mattress. The same one that crossed her face three or four times a day. The one that never failed to arouse him. She stroked him over the covers, once again firing up his passion. With a sigh he scooted over for her to join him.

"At least we'll both die satisfied," she said with a wicked smile. As she wrapped her hand around his rapidly hardening flesh, he let loose a low growl of his own.

Oh, the sacrifices a man had to make to keep his wife happy.

C３

They were going to have a mystery date. Faith couldn't be more excited if she were seventeen years old. Ryan told her he'd pick her up at eight, and to wear comfortable, casual clothing.

And then he told her to wait for him out front, instead of inside.

What was the man up to?

She was about to find out as she saw headlights coming up the drive.

That wasn't his car. It was a big SUV.

Ryan pulled around the circular drive and hopped out to open the car door.

"Good evening, wife," he said with a boyish grin.

Though he'd said the word before—wife—it held new meaning now. Before it had seemed fake. After making love with Ryan, it seemed real.

"Evening, husband," she replied. "Where are we going?"

"It's a surprise. Hop in."

She slid inside, running her hands over the leather seats. The vehicle had every gadget imaginable inside. If it were any bigger they could live in it. "Whose SUV is this?"

He shrugged. "Ours. I bought it today. Like it?"

She looked around. "Yes, but it's huge." She met his amused gaze. "You bought it today? Why?"

"I needed it for our date tonight."

"You needed it for...you bought this monstrous vehicle just for our date?"

"Uh huh."

She couldn't begin to imagine why they needed a house on wheels. What on earth did he have planned for tonight?

He kept her guessing as they drove outside the city to a neighboring town, fairly small by Las Vegas standards. More like a bedroom community, where all the amenities of suburban life could be found.

Like a drive-in movie.

She'd never have guessed it. "You're kidding."

"No, I'm not. Have you ever been to a drive-in?"

"Of course I have," she lied.

"Really." He cast her a dubious look. "When?"

"Uhh..."

"I thought so." He pulled into a spot near the rear, centering them in front of the screen. He kissed her cheek. "You know I love to be the one to give you all these firsts."

She shivered as his breath tickled her ear. The warmth in his voice held a promise she had grown accustomed to hearing.

They had popcorn, soda and a candy bar. He made her feel like a teenager on her first date. The movie began, and he held her hand. It was a date movie, about a couple obviously wrong for each other. They surmounted incredible odds, including their own stubborn hearts, until they finally realized their love and couldn't live without the other.

Faith was into it, enjoying every romantic moment.

Until suddenly a hand snaked to her breast and squeezed gently.

"Ryan!"

He laughed. "Would you like to go make out in the backseat?"

"You can't be serious."

He inched closer, sliding his hand along her thigh, his lascivious grin making her laugh.

"Aww c'mon, baby," he teased. "Just a little kiss. You know I'll respect you in the morning."

How could she resist an offer like that? His outrageous charm thrilled her. "Well, okay, but only if you promise to behave."

They hurriedly crawled into the roomy backseat, and Faith was surprised to find herself actually feeling shy. As if she really were a teenager in the throes of her first romance.

But then reality took hold as Ryan gathered her in his arms and lowered his mouth to hers.

She sighed and let herself be swept away. By the romance, the thrill, the heart-shattering intensity of his ever deepening kiss. Her mind numbly registered the movie's dialogue. The hero and heroine confessed their love for each other, and how foolish they'd been to ever think that one could live without the other.

She felt the same way.

Ryan pressed her back onto the leather seat and slid on top of her, smiling in the dark, his eyes gleaming with anticipation. Her thoughts ran rampant. What if someone walked by? The windows were tinted—no one could see. What if someone heard? The movie was loud enough to block out any sounds from other vehicles. What if...

Oh, the hell with it.

She wound her legs around his back and pulled him against her moistening heat. In desperate need, she wrestled with untucking his shirt until, with one hand, he yanked it over his head. She buried her hands in the crisp curls on his chest, her fingertips lightly grazing his hardening nipples.

He sucked in a breath and crashed down on her, crushing her delightfully with his weight. He moved against her, the feeling so erotic because they were still partly clothed, almost as if they were doing something they shouldn't.

Actually, they *were* doing something they shouldn't. Which made it all the more thrilling.

His hands roamed her body, over her clothes, flicking her nipples with the tips of his fingers, then with just a gentle touch, caressing them with his fingertips. She died in ecstasy. The heat of his hands seared through her thin bra and tank top. He followed his touch with his mouth, cupping her breasts between his lips. His hot tongue melted through her clothes, flaming her senses until she was delirious.

"Ryan, please."

He leaned back and swept his gaze over her, his breathing as ragged as hers. "What do you want, Faith?"

She reached for the waistband of his shorts. No zipper, thankfully. She tugged them down over his hips and he grinned at her.

"Want me?"

"Yes," she managed through rapid breaths. "Now, Ryan. Now."

He met her demands with fervor, yanking her shorts down and throwing them on the floor along with his own.

There wasn't even time to completely undress. She needed him, wanted him, right now.

With a savage groan he plunged inside her, covering her moans with his mouth. His tongue matched his movements, driving her wild with soul-shattering sensation.

She tightened her legs around him and rose to meet his every thrust until they were both drenched in sweat and racing toward the finish line together.

With a muffled gasp she buried her face in his neck and moaned his name as her orgasm hit with furious intensity, carrying him along with her in a fantastic rush of pleasure.

Their sweat-soaked bodies clung to each other. With Ryan still on top of her, Faith was unable to move.

The night, the date, the lovemaking—everything was perfect. Ryan had become utterly unpredictable, and never ceased to surprise her.

He feathered light kisses against her brow and touched her lips gently. "How about a hot dog? I'm starving."

She laughed, her heart full of love for the man who'd changed her world.

Ryan had no idea how the movie ended. Nor did they ever get that hot dog. But Faith exclaimed with great pride that they were now experts on lovemaking at the drive-in.

They walked into the house well after midnight, still laughing over their fumbling attempts to find their clothes which had somehow scattered from the back to the front of the SUV.

"Looks like you two had a good evening."

James stood in the entryway, glaring at them.

"Did we stay out past curfew?" Ryan was in too good a mood to be irritated by his cousin. The evening with Faith had turned out better than even he could have imagined.

"Hardly," James said with a thinly disguised sneer. "Just got in myself. So where were you off to tonight?"

"We went to the drive-in," Faith said.

James raised a brow. "Really? Whatever for?"

She turned to Ryan and they both broke out in a fit of laughter.

"To see a movie, of course," she replied, muffling her giggles behind her hand.

"And what movie was that?"

They walked past him and headed upstairs arm in arm.

"I don't recall," she said and waved goodnight.

Ryan stopped to watch her sway into their bedroom, remembering the feel of that sassy behind in his hands, the way she moaned and wiggled and...damn he'd had a great time tonight.

He'd meant it to be fun for her, because she deserved it after putting up with him for so long. And she'd made his life enjoyable for the first time in...well, forever.

Before Faith, Ryan's life hadn't been about having fun. Grandfather had no use for *joi de vivre*. Fun was closing a deal, or expanding the business, not frivolity and play.

Tonight he'd played and enjoyed every minute of it. But what he'd also gotten was a hot, passionate encounter with his wife that had his heart, not to mention all his male parts, doing flips. Who'd have thought that shy, prim Faith would turn into such a wildcat?

Ryan looked down to see James staring up at them. His cousin didn't look happy at all.

Ah, yes. The perfect end to a perfect evening.

CB

Faith left the doctor's office and flopped onto a bench outside the medical building. She needed a minute to get her mind functioning normally again. Right now she was too numb to even think about getting in the car.

She was pregnant. A month along already.

How had it happened so fast? Ryan had told her he was plenty fertile. That was an understatement. Judging from her calculations she had gotten pregnant the first night they'd made love, or immediately thereafter.

She cracked a smile, followed by a full-fledged grin. Anyone walking by might think she was crazy, sitting on a bench alone smiling into space.

Who cared? She was pregnant! She and the man she loved had created a child. She'd remember this day for the rest of her life, remember the feeling of exquisite joy that had settled over her when the doctor had given her the news. Oh, she'd suspected it for a couple weeks, but didn't want to get her hopes up. Not until the doc gave her the official word.

But along with joy came trepidation. What did her pregnancy mean for her relationship with Ryan? She remembered James's words that day in the kitchen.

You know he's going to dump you as soon as he gets you pregnant.

She hadn't believed him. Wouldn't believe him. She'd seen the change in Ryan over the past couple months. He enjoyed himself more, smiled more. Seemed happy. With her.

Faith was beginning to hope that maybe this marriage could work out. Maybe it wasn't just an agreement on paper, but an agreement of two hearts.

Admittedly, for her it had always been personal. Maybe it had become that way for Ryan, too. He'd never said anything to her to lead her to believe he might want to make their marriage permanent. It was more the way he acted around her. She hoped her intuition was right.

Now she just had to find him and tell him about the baby. Then she'd see how he felt about it. But somehow, in her soul, she knew he cared for her, knew he wouldn't kick her out.

She drove home carefully, conscious of the precious cargo she carried. She rushed into the house, threw her purse down and went searching for her husband.

He wasn't in his office, nor was he in their room. She ran into James as she headed back into the kitchen.

"Have you seen Ryan?" she asked.

He shook his head. "Not recently. Why?"

"I was looking for him. I need to talk to him about something."

"Anything I can help you with?"

"No. No, thank you." She didn't have time to sit around and play word games with James. She wanted to talk to Ryan.

"I think he mentioned he was going to be at the office tonight. Something about a meeting there and he'd be working late."

"The office? He didn't tell me about a meeting." Then again, she'd been so distracted and nervous about her doctor's appointment she may not have heard him.

"Maybe you should meet him there," James suggested.

"Maybe I will." She thanked James and decided to clean up, dress nice, and surprise Ryan at the office later. Then she'd take him out to dinner and tell him the news.

She smiled on her way up the stairs. It was going to be a memorable day.

It was well after eight by the time Faith reached the office. She parked outside and had the guard let her in.

The office was dark when she entered the main door. She followed the dimly lit hallway to the executive offices, the only area on the floor with lights on.

She tiptoed into the outer office where her desk was located. She heard voices and immediately pushed aside the disappointing thought that Ryan hadn't concluded his business yet. She was practically bursting with the news.

Nevertheless, she'd wait him out. He was going to be so happy when he heard. She sat at her desk and pulled a few files to work on while she waited.

It took a few moments, but Faith finally tuned into the conversation inside. Her ears perked up at the sound of a decidedly feminine voice.

"Well, how much longer is this going to take?"

A heated rush overcame her. She'd know that whining voice anywhere. It was Erica Stanton, Ryan's former fiancée.

Faith couldn't believe Erica had the audacity to show up after what she'd done to Ryan. Ready to defend her husband, she rose from her desk and started for the door, then stopped as she peeked inside the half open doorway. Ryan's back was to her, but Erica had her arms wrapped around his neck, trailing her fingers through his dark hair.

"You know I hate waiting, darling. This whole charade has been miserable from the start. Thank heavens that idiot secretary of yours fell for it, hook, line and sinker. To think you had to endure having sex with that pitifully plain creature! I can only imagine the hardships you've had to endure."

Faith's world turned a hazy red as the impact of the woman's words sunk in. Erica was talking about her! She grabbed hold of the doorway for support, trying to will the lightheadedness to pass.

Ryan bent over Erica's ear and whispered. She couldn't hear what he said, but Erica whined so loud it was easy to figure out at least one side of the conversation.

She waited for Ryan to push the woman away.

He didn't. In fact, he slid his arms around Erica's waist, pulling her closer to him.

This wasn't real. It couldn't be happening.

"I know, darling," Erica said, her lips perfecting a well-practiced pout. "But at least we won't be saddled with a brat that neither of us want. As soon as you get the little mouse pregnant, you can divorce her and we can be together. Then we'll have everything we want. All without a child, and without the restrictions of your grandfather's will."

Erica leaned up on her tiptoes and buried her face in Ryan's neck. He pulled her even closer against him.

Faith's knees buckled and she leaned against the doorway, trying to quell the rapid breaths. She felt dizzy, disoriented and utterly sick.

She had to get out of there before they saw her. Before she said something, did something to alert them of her presence.

Fighting the rising bile in her throat she grabbed her purse and stumbled down the hallway. The elevators seemed miles away, despite the fact she was almost running.

She couldn't breathe, the tightness in her chest constricting her lungs. Tears blinded her visual progress towards the elevators and she held onto the wall to guide her.

Just a few feet and she'd be there. She had to make it despite the knife-like pain ripping her heart to pieces.

The elevator door opened and she hurried inside, furiously wiping the tears away, hoping against hope that neither Ryan nor Erica had seen her.

It took forever for the elevator to make its lengthy trek to the lobby. She shifted on both feet and paced the slow-moving box, trying to think. Her mind wouldn't cooperate. She didn't know what to do next.

Was it possible to feel like this and survive? Miserable, lonely emptiness shuddered through her. Knowing she had been used, knowing now that he had never loved her or even cared for her.

Finally, the lobby. She walked with a brisk pace past the guard, waving at his acknowledgement but unable to face him. She slid into her car and sat there, trying to control her breathing.

She had to focus. Had to gather her wits about her. It wouldn't do her any good to drive in this condition.

After all, she had someone else beside herself to think about.

Their baby. Correction—her baby. Ryan hadn't wanted this child any more than he'd wanted her.

How could she have been so stupid? How could she have let her love for him blind her to his real feelings?

If the whole situation wasn't so pathetic she'd laugh.

First thing to do would be to go home. No, she corrected herself. Not home. To the McKay mansion.

That had never been her home. She'd have to find another.

Another with ample space for her and her child.

Chapter Twelve

Ryan had paced the bedroom for well over an hour. He was tired of waiting, of worrying.

Where was Faith?

He'd come home from a downtown meeting with a potential client, only to find his wife gone. No note, no message.

It was after ten.

Panic had set in right away.

He'd told himself he was being ridiculous. She was probably out shopping and would be home soon. But usually she called him if she was going somewhere.

And she wasn't answering her cell phone.

It wasn't like Faith to leave without a word.

He sat on the bed and forced himself to think logically. He bent his head to massage his temples. Then he started to laugh.

If anyone saw him like this they'd swear it was someone else, not the cool and calm Ryan McKay.

The cool and calm Ryan McKay didn't care about anyone. He refused to get involved, would never open his heart. He was cold, unfeeling.

And one hundred and ten percent in love with his wife.

He lay back on the bed and contemplated the ceiling.

He was in love. With Faith.

So much for not getting personal. He'd made it as personal as it could get. He'd opened his heart and let her in.

And now he that he had let her in, he wanted to keep her there.

Forever.

He had a sneaking suspicion that when he told her he loved her, she'd return the words to him. For the first time, *happily ever after* didn't seem as far-fetched as he once thought.

Maybe it hadn't worked for his parents. Maybe his grandfather hadn't known how to express his love. That didn't mean Ryan had to follow in their footsteps. Faith had given him the one thing he'd never had before, the one thing he now craved more than anything else.

Love. Unconditional love.

He jumped off the bed at the sound of the front door.

"Faith?" He called out from the top of the stairs.

No answer, but he saw her heading up.

"Are you all right? I've been worried about you."

It looked like he had been right to be worried. Dried tears streaked her face and she walked right past him without a word.

He followed her into the bedroom, his heartbeat accelerating. "What's wrong?"

No response. She didn't even look at him, just headed for the dressing area. He trailed behind her, concern conjuring up images of her wrecking the car or being in pain. He stopped her progress into the closet by gently reaching for her arm. "Faith. Turn around and talk to me. What happened?"

She faced him and he took a step back at the daggers in her blue eyes. They'd darkened like a hurricane sky, and yet underneath held a sadness that pierced his heart.

"Nothing happened, Ryan."

Her voice was flat. No emotion. That wasn't like Faith at all.

"That's bull. You're clearly upset. What's wrong? Did James say something to you?"

She dragged out a suitcase and laid it on the table in the closet. "No, James didn't say anything to me."

"What are you doing?"

"Packing."

"What are you packing for?"

"I'm leaving."

His heart stopped. "What do you mean you're leaving?"

Pain etched creases on her forehead and she shook her head at him. "This isn't working out."

Dread formed in the pit of his stomach. "What?"

"I can't stay here any longer, Ryan. I...I just can't."

He reached for her but she pulled away, shooting him an icy look. Ryan threaded his hands through his hair. Her behavior made no sense at all. "Come out here, talk to me."

She shook her head and continued packing. "There's nothing to talk about. I really tried, but I'm just not interested in continuing this charade."

"Charade?" He threaded his finger over his brow in an attempt to erase the budding headache. "I don't understand this at all. Something's happened to upset you. Tell me what it is."

She shrugged as if she didn't care at all. He knew better.

"I just don't want to be here anymore. I'm tired of being your pawn, Ryan. Tired of being molded and turned into someone who isn't me." She threw a few additional things in her suitcase and closed it, the snap of the locks echoing with the finality of a closing prison door.

She picked up the suitcase, barely filled with more than a few items of clothing, and headed back into the bedroom.

"I'll be taking Tiger with me as soon as I get settled somewhere. Please ask Margaret to look after him for me until I send word."

This was ridiculous. He did grab her then, gently so as not to jar her, but with a firm grip despite the lifeless look she gave him. "I'm not letting you leave. Not without an explanation."

She opened her mouth as if she'd say something, then clamped it shut.

"Faith, tell me what's wrong."

"Let go of me."

He dropped his hand. She straightened her blouse and took a breath. "You want an explanation? Here's the only one you'll get from me. I'm a person, Ryan. With a heart—with feelings. Not someone you can toy with, use to amuse yourself and then discard when I've served your purposes. I may not be much to look at, and maybe I let my mother's voice dwell in my head for too many years, but I am worthy of love. And I don't deserve this."

"Deserve what?" He heard the rise in his voice, but couldn't stop it. He was frustrated and getting angrier by the minute. He'd been guilty of many things in the past, things he didn't want to think about even now. He'd hurt people without thinking. But Faith—he hadn't done a thing to hurt her. And yet the way she looked at him, her eyes so full of pain and misery, made him feel guilty.

"Don't pretend you don't know what I'm talking about, Ryan. It's insulting. And I won't even dignify it by mentioning it."

He sighed and pulled his hand through his hair. "Faith. I have no earthly idea why you're so upset. And what it is you think I've done to you? If you'll stop for a minute and talk to me we can figure it out."

For a second she seemed to consider it. Then just as quickly her eyes clouded over once again and she picked up the suitcase. "I'm sorry, Ryan. Sorry for what this will do to you, but I just can't stay here with you any longer."

She was really going to leave him. He'd been tried and convicted of whatever crime she thought he'd committed. And she wouldn't even give him an opportunity to defend himself.

Suddenly it hit him. He knew what this was about.

The new clothes, the hairstyle, the makeup, the confident attitude. Those things changed her. Now that she'd realized how much she had to offer she also discovered how much he lacked.

She didn't care at all about him. She wanted out.

It was simple, and oh-so-clear.

He followed her down the steps and stopped her when she got to the bottom. "I see what's happening here."

She turned. "Do you?"

He refused to buy the sad look in her eyes. It was an act, and one he'd seen countless times in the past. Frankly, he was surprised she was so cold and calculated, but then again hadn't everyone he cared about done this to him?

"Yes. It's obvious. You become an attractive butterfly and suddenly decide you want to spread those pretty little wings and fly away to the outside world, see what's out there that's better than what you have here."

Her words sliced at him. "That's ridiculous!"

"Is it? Then explain why you suddenly decide to leave, when you would have done anything I asked you before...before you—"

She finished it for him. "Before you transformed me?"

"Yes." That's not what he meant at all, but if she thought so, more the better.

"That's priceless, Ryan. Obviously, this is your pathetic attempt to remove any guilt from your own shoulders and place it on mine. Yes, you had this planned all so well didn't you? Except this time you aren't going to win. This time I'm not playing the game."

She picked up the suitcase and opened the front door.

"Go ahead, Faith. Run. Run to your new lover or your new life or whatever it is out there you think is better than what you have right here."

But she didn't hear him as the door slammed shut before he could finish his sentence.

The silence was deafening. He stood in the foyer, the dark closing in, the emptiness pervading the very air around him.

Okay, she was gone. Good riddance. He should have known better than to open his heart.

Suddenly, he was the small boy again who was told Daddy was too busy to play with him. Daddy was gone now. Mommy was gone now. And Grandfather had no use for an emotionally distraught child.

He'd learned then not to love anyone. Love stabbed holes in your heart, and your soul bled through them. It hurt when you loved someone. Because they never loved you back.

Ryan had made a fatal mistake. He'd fallen in love with Faith, and handed her the power to hurt him.

He'd buried hurt before. He could do it again.

❧

She couldn't sit still. The hotel room was like a tiny box, imprisoning her. She wanted to go home.

But where was home? She didn't have one anymore.

How could she have been so blind? How could she have allowed Ryan to creep into her heart, only to find he was playing her? She shouldn't be surprised by that.

Her mother's voice rang in her ears, those punishing lectures she'd heard over and over and over again. Men would hurt her. She was plain and homely and no man would ever love her.

For so long she hadn't wanted to believe it. But her mother had been right.

How Ryan and Erica must have been laughing over her these past months. She was so naïve. When would she learn?

And since she'd left, not a word from him. It had been days, and not a single word. Did she really expect he would try and find her? He was probably glad she was gone.

Of course, she hadn't gone to the office. She'd have to find another job now. There was no way she could continue to work for him, not after everything that had happened.

And then there was the baby.

The only bright spot in this whole dismal affair.

The twin towers of The Chalet Hotel shone like a beacon from her hotel window. She wondered how Ryan would feel if he knew she had taken up residence in one of the competing chains.

She hadn't even asked for a suite, even though she had a considerable expense account as Ryan's wife. She wasn't going to touch his money.

As soon as she got back on her feet, found a new job and a new place to live, she'd never use another dime of McKay money.

They'd divorce, and she'd get nothing. After all, she'd left before the terms of the contract were met. That meant she'd go away empty-handed.

Of course, she could tell him about the baby. Then he'd keep the company and she'd be entitled to a settlement. But she'd have to live with him, sleep with him, for the remainder of the year. No way would she do that. Her heart couldn't take it.

Besides, that would mean he'd won. And so would Erica. And they would spend the rest of their lives laughing at her stupidity.

She'd be damned if he was going to win this one. Let him lose McKay Corporation. That was his one great love anyway. Let him feel a bit of the pain she was going through right now, knowing how it felt to lose something he loved.

Despite losing control of the company, he'd still be wealthy. He could start something new. She pushed aside the nagging guilt that nestled in her stomach. She wouldn't feel guilty. This wasn't her fault.

And in the meantime, she'd look for another job. With a company that wouldn't mind her taking a bit of time off for maternity leave. And she and her child would be fine.

Her heart would heal. Eventually.

A knock at the door interrupted her self-pity session. She opened it, her jaw dropping as Leland Banks stood there. How in the world had he found her?

Margaret, of course. She was the only one who knew where Faith had gone.

"Margaret told you I was here."

He nodded as she opened the door and led him into the tiny living area. "Yes."

She motioned him to the small sofa. "What can I do for you, Leland?"

"Come back, ma'am."

She shook her head. "I can't. My marriage to Ryan is over."

"I think I know why you would think it was over, but I must tell you you're wrong."

"No, you don't know why, although I appreciate you coming. You can just go back to Ryan and tell him I'm not coming back, and I'm sorry he's going to lose the company."

"He doesn't care about the company, Mrs. McKay. He's already called a board meeting for noon today to announce the end of your marriage."

She frowned. "You'd think he'd wait until the board called a meeting to check on the status of our marriage. Why the hurry?"

"He's very unhappy, ma'am."

Right. He was probably unhappy about losing the company, not about losing Faith.

"His happiness is no longer my problem, Leland." She turned her head to the window, swiping away the hair falling in front of her face.

"He loves you."

She whipped around, desperately needing to refute Leland's statement. "That's a lie!"

Leland remained stoic, unmoved by her passionate denial. "He loves you."

Tears threatened, but Faith refused to be swayed. "He's a good actor, Leland. He even fooled me."

"You don't understand, ma'am. I know why you left. If you'll just let me explain—"

"Explain what? Explain how upset poor Ryan is at the thought of losing his company?" She crossed her arms, hoping to hold in the wretched grief threatening to pour out. "How much is he paying you to come here and beg on his behalf?"

Leland sniffed and stood. "That's insulting."

She shrugged and waved her hand. "Just tell him it didn't work, Leland. I'm not interested in hearing any more." How much more could she stand? She felt stupid enough as it was. Couldn't this just end?

"I beg your pardon, ma'am, but you're just going to have to listen to me!"

She turned, never having heard Leland raise his voice before. He stood rigid in the middle of the room, but his brow was furrowed and anger crossed his normally implacable features.

"I overheard James this morning," he said.

"So?"

"He was speaking with Miss Stanton on the telephone. Normally I don't eavesdrop, would be improper, but I paused when I heard their discussion."

Despite wanting to close her ears and her heart to his explanation, something about his statement tipped along the edges of her memory. "Go on."

"He was laughing. About you. He was talking to Miss Stanton about how they'd fooled you when they led you to believe that James was Master Ryan. James said their plan worked perfectly, that you moved out that evening."

No. That's not how it happened. She wouldn't believe it. It *was* Ryan that night. She'd heard him, saw him with her own eyes.

Or had she?

"I went to the office last week to surprise Ryan," she explained. "I found him with Erica, their arms around each other. Laughing at how gullible I was."

Leland's brown eyes softened. "Did you see Master Ryan's face?"

She thought. Ryan's back had been turned to her the entire time. "No, just his back."

"And did he speak?"

"Yes, but come to think of it, I only heard him mumble because he whispered in Erica's ear."

Suddenly the room spun wildly. Faith grasped the sofa for support and reached for Leland's hand. "Oh, no. Oh, Leland. Did they trick me?"

His expression softened as he coaxed her into a seat. "It appears so."

Shock, hurt, guilt and anger all swirled inside her. How could she have done this to Ryan? How could she have done this to them?

How could James and Erica have done this? Damn them!

She buried her face in her hands, unable to believe what she'd allowed to occur. Her lack of belief in herself had screwed everything up. She couldn't keep the tears at bay and finally broke down. Leland gathered her in his arms and held her against him as she poured out her grief.

When she had no tears left to expend, he handed her a handkerchief. She laughed.

"It seems you're always here when I fall apart."

He nodded, his voice soft and paternal. "I don't mind, really. Margaret and I always wanted children, and Master Ryan was the closest we ever had. But he never allowed anyone to love him."

She looked at him, the realization hitting her before the words were out of his mouth.

"Until you," he said with a smile.

Oh, no. What had she done? "Leland, I've made a terrible mistake. I've hurt Ryan deeply."

"No, ma'am, the mistake was made by James and Miss Stanton. They manipulated you and Mr. McKay. And now you and he are at odds, and he's prepared to give up McKay Corporation."

Anger and desperation filled her. She'd caused irreparable damage, and all because she believed that Ryan couldn't really love her. Damn James—he'd known it, too.

"Leland, how bad is Ryan?"

He shook his head. "Mr. McKay—Ryan—is not good. He mopes about, has barely gone to the office, won't speak to anyone. It's quite obvious he hasn't slept or eaten much since you left. He's trying to be indifferent about it, but he's hurting."

The pain was nearly unbearable. She wanted to run home to Ryan, throw her arms around him and beg his forgiveness. Then she wanted to tell him how much she loved him, how much she'd always loved him. And let him know about the baby.

The baby!

She looked at her watch. "What time is the board meeting?"

"Noon. Why?"

"I have to hurry."

"What are you doing, ma'am?"

She should have believed in Ryan, instead of letting her mother's words seep back into her consciousness. She'd let her own insecurities rule her judgment. Now she'd lost her chance at love.

But she could still make amends to Ryan, at least professionally.

Faith grabbed Leland's hands. "I've got to save the company for Ryan! Help me, Leland, we have to make it on time!"

Chapter Thirteen

Ryan stood in front of the Board of Directors, a sense of dismal finality darkening his mood even more than it had been lately. This would be the last time he'd stand before them as CEO. Less than a week ago everything looked as if it would work out. Hell, less than a week ago he hadn't cared a whit about goings-on at the company. All he'd cared about was Faith and his realization that he loved her.

Now everything he'd cared about was gone.

There was no point in delaying the inevitable. Faith had left him before the year was up, before she'd gotten pregnant, before they'd made a life together. A real life. The terms of the will hadn't been fulfilled.

James had won.

And James knew it too, judging from the self-satisfied smirk on his face. It killed Ryan to turn this company over to James, knowing his cousin had no intention of keeping it intact. He'd probably have it on the market within a week, selling it off in chunks to the highest bidder.

It hurt more than Ryan dared to admit. Not the loss of his job, he didn't really care about that. But the loss of the McKay holdings, the company his grandfather and great grandfather had built from nothing. Ryan had made plans for bigger and better things in the future.

Now all was lost.

A few months ago, the thought of losing control of the company would have devastated him. Now, all he could think about was Faith.

"Will we be starting soon?" Lincoln Simmons, one of the directors, looked at his watch. "It is after twelve, you know, and I have another meeting to attend."

Ryan took a deep breath. He'd stood in front of this board thousands of times and had never once been nervous. Today, his pulse raced, his gut felt like he'd swallowed a basketball and his head throbbed. Might as well get it over with.

What was he waiting for? A miracle? An angel to swoop down and make everything right?

It wasn't going to happen. Ryan didn't believe in miracles.

"Yes, let's begin." He cleared his throat, took a sip of water, and began. "As you all know, Quentin McKay outlined specific terms in his will relating to my ability to hold my position as CEO and majority owner of McKay Corporation."

"Yes, yes, we know all this stuff. Just get on with it."

All eyes turned to James. He wasn't liked by any of the board members. At least Ryan could take some satisfaction in that. They stared at his improper outburst.

James looked around the board room and slinked further into his chair.

"Continue, Ryan," Stan said, his eyes full of compassion.

"I married Faith Lewis over three months ago, with the intent of fulfilling my obligations related to my grandfather's will. The stipulations indicated that Faith and I must remain married, and within one year produce a pregnancy."

"You're stating the obvious," James interrupted. "We all know what the will required. Get on with it."

Ryan seethed with an anger he couldn't turn on his cousin. Oh, but he'd really like to. Instead, for the few minutes he retained control of the company, he'd make him suffer.

"If you don't mind, James, I am CEO of this company and majority stockholder. Either hold your comments until I'm through or I'll have you removed from the room."

James opened his mouth to speak, then looked around at the hostile faces at the table. Ryan suppressed a grin. Apparently James wasn't as stupid as he thought. He clamped his mouth shut and shot an evil glare at Ryan.

Not that it mattered. In mere minutes Ryan would be the one out the door, and James, God help them all, would take over.

Ryan swallowed. "I have an announcement to make. It's necessary for you all to be made aware that—"

"That the terms of the will are even closer to fulfillment," Faith said, loud enough for everyone in the room to hear. All heads turned in her direction.

Faith's dramatic entrance through the double doors at the back of the boardroom shocked everyone into silence, especially Ryan, who stared dumfounded at her. She stopped as soon as she entered, drawing deep breaths as if she'd run all the way up the stairs to the twenty-first floor of McKay Towers.

Ryan's heart pounded like crazy. He didn't know whether to be happy or supremely angry to see her.

What the hell was she doing here? And why now? Had she come to gloat over his failure?

She cautiously approached the front of the room and stood next to Ryan, smiling at him as if they hadn't argued, hadn't dissolved their relationship. What was going on?

The next shock to his system came when she slipped her hand inside his and squeezed.

"Please, trust me," she whispered into his ear. "I'm sorry, I'll explain in a minute."

Ryan leaned back and searched her face, looking for some explanation. Her cheeks were flushed and her eyes glazed with excitement and something else. Hope?

She'd asked him to trust her. How could he? He'd placed his heart in her hands, and look what she'd done.

Their eyes remained locked for a few more seconds. Faith refused to look away, despite Ryan's penetrating stare.

It didn't matter, anyway. Nothing she said or did would change things. He stepped back from the podium and let Faith have the microphone.

"My apologies for running late," she said. "I had an appointment this morning, and you know how doctors are. They don't always keep a timely schedule."

What was she up to? Her bright blue eyes sparkled with joy, and there was a glow to her face he'd seen many times, usually right after they made love.

"Do you want to tell them, my love, or should I?" she asked.

Tell who what? She'd completely lost him now. "Uhh, go ahead. You tell them."

"I'd be delighted." She turned to address the board with a wide grin. "I'm pleased to announce that Ryan and I are expecting a child."

His heart skipped a beat before pummeling his chest. What the hell was this? Had she gone insane? Ryan pulled her aside as the board members applauded and yelled congratulations. "What the hell do you think you're doing?" he hissed.

She was nonplussed, her face full of innocence. "I'm addressing the board like you asked me to."

"You can't lie to them, Faith. They'll know. I was planning to tell them about our breakup. Why are you here?"

"Please, Ryan, if you ever had any trust in me before, then give me a chance. I'll explain everything as soon as we're finished here."

"Why should I trust—"

"That's a lie!" James slapped the conference table, the sound echoing in the large room.

Once again, James quieted the room with his outburst. He stood, hands clenched into fists at his side, his face reddening.

With surprising calm, Faith placed her hand on her hip and raised her eyebrows. "Really, James. And what makes you think it's a lie?"

"Because I know you two aren't together anymore!"

"It appears to me we're together, wouldn't you agree, Ryan?"

She looked up at him with such love it stunned him. Love he knew she didn't feel for him. It was all a lie. Wasn't it?

But she'd asked him to trust her. Could he? He'd never been able to trust anyone before her. And she'd left him. Just like everyone he'd loved.

Could he take the chance?

"Oh, the hell with it," he mumbled and slid his arm around Faith's shoulder. He'd regret this later, but for now he'd play the game. "Yes, we're obviously together. I'm glad I didn't have to make the announcement without Faith present."

"And if there are any concerns about the validity of my pregnancy, I'll be happy to provide the name and telephone number of my obstetrician for verification."

"But, but..." James sputtered.

"James," Faith said casually. "You don't really want me to bring up your impersonation of Ryan to the board, do you?"

"What? What impersonation?" Ryan asked, trying to think beyond the excited whispers of the board members.

"Your cousin decided to play a little trick on me," she said, shooting a glare at James. "I found him being, shall we say, promiscuous with Erica Stanton. In your office."

The room hushed, all eyes focused on Faith's revelation.

"With Erica? When?" Ryan shot a quick look toward James. His face was reddening. Something began to boil within Ryan. The pieces of the puzzle were starting to fall into place.

"A few days ago. I came to the office to surprise you one evening, and I thought it was you. James was in your office, with her," Faith said, accenting the *her* with a decidedly feminine dislike.

Ryan couldn't believe it. Though he could believe almost anything of James. But Faith. What had she thought when she'd seen James impersonating him? Of course. That's why she'd left him!

"It's not true!" James said, his face contorted with rage and frustration.

Stan Fredericks stood. "You know the penalty for trying to manipulate the outcome of the marriage, don't you, James?"

Ryan had forgotten that little tidbit in Quentin McKay's will. Anyone who stood to gain from Ryan's departure as CEO and was found guilty of manipulating their marriage, would lose their board position.

"She can't prove a thing," James sneered.

"Oh, can't I?" Faith's eyes all but gleamed. "You know, it's amazing, but I thought Erica Stanton had more guts.

Apparently a little well-pressed inquisition and she waffled like a burst balloon. Erica will be more than happy to corroborate my accusation."

Ryan had to admit surprise at Faith's backbone. She stared James down like two starving dogs after the same bone. Who'd have thought the shy kitten could turn into a menacing tigress?

James stood and heaved breaths in and out, but didn't say a word.

"Is there something you'd like to add, James?" Ryan asked, all attempts at politeness gone.

James looked like a big red beet about to burst. Ryan wanted to laugh at him, but held himself in check. Without another word James pushed his chair back and stormed from the room.

It was over. Ryan exhaled a sigh of relief. "If there are no other questions or comments we'll adjourn the meeting, and see you next month. Thank you for coming."

Ryan had to wait through the congratulations from the board members before he could get Faith alone to question her. After everyone left they remained in the room.

"Now will you please tell me what the hell is going on? Why did you lie to the board like that?"

"I didn't lie."

"Yes, you did. You lied about the fact we were still together, and you lied about being pregnant."

Faith frowned and blushed. This wasn't the way she had planned to tell him, but then again nothing had gone as planned the past week. And most of that had been her fault.

No, it had been James's fault.

"I guess you'll have to decide the part about us being together, but the pregnancy part is true. I'm going to have your child, Ryan."

"What?"

The look on his face was priceless. Another memory to tuck away and recall fondly when she was older. "You heard me."

"You're really pregnant?"

She couldn't seem to wipe the smile off her face. "Yes, I'm really pregnant."

He seemed distracted, his thoughts miles away. "How long have you known?"

"Since the night I went to your office and found who I thought was you in Erica's arms. The night I left you."

He ran his fingers through his hair. "That's what I figured happened. I can't believe James did that."

She nodded. "I went to the doctor that day because I hadn't been feeling well, had missed my period and I was pretty sure I was pregnant, but wanted a blood test to be absolutely sure. When I found out, I came home looking for you but James said you'd be at the office until late."

"I was downtown at a client's office that day, but I was home that evening."

"I know that now. I didn't know that when I walked into the office to find Erica with her arms around someone that at the time I thought was you."

He stared dumfounded. "James and I do look alike, especially from the back."

"Yes. I just assumed it was you. Stupid of me, I know. And Erica made this speech about how the two of you fooled me, how you were going to dump me as soon as I was pregnant, and then you'd get back with her without having to raise a child."

"I'm going to kill them," he said through clenched teeth.

She touched his arm. "No, you're not. You've already beaten James. He'll never have the company now, and he knows it."

"The bastard." His face contorted in anger. Faith touched his shoulder and he flinched and turned to her.

"You thought I'd cheat on you with Erica."

She shook her head. "I...I didn't know what to believe."

"Why didn't you tell me? Confront me with it instead of just packing up and leaving? Why didn't you have a little trust in me?"

Panic rose up in her throat. "I...I didn't think you wanted me."

"Why in hell would you think that?" He jammed his fingers through his hair. "Damn, Faith, couldn't you read me? Couldn't you tell how I felt about you? How could you have just left me without explanation?"

She fell into the nearest chair and clasped her shaking hands together. How could she explain to him that she didn't think he'd want her, that it was easier to believe he'd rather run back to Erica than make a life with her? That night, she'd been on the verge of blurting out that she'd seen him with Erica. But a lifetime of hearing her mother's voice in her head, of having to face her mother's disapproving looks...no, she just couldn't go through that with the man she loved. So she'd taken the coward's way out and just walked away, making the biggest mistake of her life.

"I see," he said, jamming papers into his briefcase.

"Ryan, please. Let me explain."

He looked down at her, his eyes bleak and remote. "Like you let me explain the night you left? You've done your part,

Faith. You got pregnant. Thank you for coming to my rescue here, but I think we've said all we're going to say. It's clear you'll never trust in me and you don't have the feelings I thought you had. I won't live like that."

He turned and walked out of the room. Faith's body weighed like cement, making her unable to move, to go after him.

She'd hurt him. The one thing he'd always been able to count on was her trust and loyalty to him. And then when he'd needed it the most she'd let him down. She hadn't believed him. Could she blame him for not believing her now?

It didn't matter. None of this mattered. She'd made amends and saved McKay Corporation, but she couldn't win back the man she loved.

C3

Ryan slammed the front door and threw his briefcase on the table. He stormed into his office and shut the door, heading straight for the bar to get a drink.

Downing two quick shots, he welcomed the burn in his chest. Anything to kill the pain.

A soft knock sounded at the door.

"Go away!" he bellowed.

"Master Ryan, may I come in?"

"Not now, Leland. Whatever it is can wait." Ryan threw off his jacket and slid down onto the leather sofa, leaning his head back and closing his eyes.

Anther drink, that's what he needed. Dull the pain, send him into oblivion, make him forget.

The click of the door opening had him jumping up off the sofa. "I said I didn't want to be disturbed."

Leland stepped in and closed the door behind him. Ryan glared at his butler.

"I'm sorry, sir, but you really must listen to me."

Leland had never disobeyed an order before. In all the time Ryan had known him, he'd been the epitome of professionalism. In fact, he'd just noticed that Leland had called him *Master Ryan.* He hadn't done that since he was a boy.

"What is it?" Ryan stepped to the bar and poured another drink.

"Drinking won't make you forget her." Leland stood in the center of the room, his hands clasped behind him.

"Don't know what you're talking about," Ryan said, reaching for the bottle.

In two quick steps Leland grasped the bottle and pulled it away. If Ryan hadn't seen it with his own eyes he wouldn't have believed it. Nor could he believe the disapproving look Leland gave him.

"You've had enough alcohol," Leland said, slipping the bottle onto a shelf.

"Do not tell me what to do," Ryan ground out, his teeth clenched together so hard his jaw throbbed.

"Someone needs to tell you what to do. I'm tired of seeing one McKay after another make a royal mess of their lives. I allowed your father to do it but I will not permit you to make the same mistakes."

What in the world? Ryan was speechless. Leland advanced on him and Ryan backed up a step, unable to fathom this new side of the family butler.

"Leland, what the—"

"Enough." Leland held up a hand to silence Ryan. "Mrs. McKay loves you. She's always loved you. The fact you are too afraid to let her is something that I will not allow. This has to stop somewhere, and this is as good a place as any."

Ryan sat back down. Leland stood over him, his dark eyes fierce with anger.

"I watched what your father and mother and grandfather did to you. Watched them manipulate you and treat you like nothing but one of McKay Corporation's assets. Watched a sensitive, wonderful young boy grow up without any love or affection."

How could Leland have noticed all these things? Ryan had felt so isolated, so alone, and yet as he thought about it, Leland and Margaret's kindness toward him had been the one bright thing in his childhood.

"I've loved you since you were an infant, Master Ryan. Margaret and I both have. You have a capability to love, despite your denials. You have shown love to Mrs. McKay in ways that made me incredibly proud of you. But now, when she needs you the most, you've let her down."

"I let her down? Now wait a minute, Leland." Ryan began to stand up, but Leland pushed his shoulder until he sat.

"Stay there, I'm not finished."

Ryan was too surprised to move.

"As I was saying, both Margaret and I love you. You are the child we never could have. Of course with our stations we could not show you parental love. It saddened us that we couldn't give you the love you so desperately needed, but we were heartened when Mrs. McKay came into your life. Finally, we thought someone loved you the way you deserved to be loved. We couldn't show you, but she could."

The revelations tore at his gut. Leland and Margaret loved him? Had loved him, all his life? And Faith loved him?

Was he so wrapped up in the hurts of the past, so insistent on refusing any kind of love, that he'd missed everything?

"I had no idea, Leland. I'm sorry." He stood, stepping towards the man who'd been more parent to him than any McKay ever could.

Leland placed his hand on Ryan's shoulder, and Ryan could swear he saw moisture gather in the old man's eyes. "The McKays have made a mess of love for many years...Ryan. See if you can't change that now. With Faith. She loves you."

That was the first time Ryan ever heard Leland use their first names. "Faith doesn't—"

"Don't think with your head on this, Ryan. Think with your heart. You know she loves you. Don't let her slip through your fingers or you'll regret it until the day you die."

CB

Faith hoped she wouldn't run into anyone at the office. She'd sailed past the guard with what little bravado she possessed, hoping he wouldn't see through her misery and pain.

She wanted to pack up and take her personal things out of the office before Ryan came in. With any luck, she'd slip out before any McKay Corporation employees showed up for work.

After the showdown in the conference room yesterday, Faith had gone back to the hotel and waited, hoping that Ryan would change his mind and come to her.

He hadn't.

It was over. She'd tried her best to make amends, and it hadn't worked. He didn't love her enough to forgive her.

Fighting the tears blurring her vision, she dug into the bottom drawer of her desk for the last of her things.

"What do you think you're doing?"

She jumped at the sound of Ryan's voice. Damn. Damn, damn, damn! This wasn't supposed to happen. She swatted at the tears with the back of her sleeve and turned around.

"I'm sorry," she said, barely able to find her voice. "I had thought to have this done before you arrived."

He looked so good, his jeans snug against his well-muscled body, the dark polo shirt bringing out the fire in those stormy eyes she loved so well. She fought back the aching sob that threatened to escape.

Ryan's gaze traveled to the box on top of her desk. "Going somewhere?"

She nodded, unable to speak.

"I don't want you to go," he said, his voice barely above a whisper.

Her eyes met his and she couldn't believe what she saw there. Determination and something warm and tender that just about ripped her heart in two.

"You don't?" she said, swallowing hard.

He shook his head. "I'm a stupid fool. Thank God Leland had the sense to point that out to me."

"Leland did?"

"Yeah, believe it or not. The old man laid down the law to me last night. It was like having a father. A real father."

She saw the hint of a smile on his face, and her heart swelled with hope and love. "He loves you, you know."

Then the smile appeared in full. "Yeah, I sort of got that idea."

Faith grinned. "I knew he did. And I hoped that some day you two would realize that you're more father and son than butler and employer."

Ryan stepped toward her. "My eyes were opened last night, Faith. To many things. The least of which is how badly I treated you."

"It wasn't you, Ryan, it was me. I believed the man in your office that night with Erica was you. I should have known better."

He grabbed her hands and pulled her against him, holding her tight. "An easy mistake to make. No wonder you were so upset that night. How did you find out it was James?"

"Leland overheard him on the phone with Erica, and he told me what happened. I'm sorry, too, Ryan, for the way I treated you that night. It was supposed to be perfect. I was going to tell you about the baby, tell you how much I loved you and ask if you wanted to stay married to me."

His eyes widened. "You were going to tell me you loved me?"

She nodded. "Of course I love you. I've loved you since the day I met you. I want a life with you, Ryan. A real marriage, not a business arrangement. But only if that's what you want, too."

He turned his head sideways as if evaluating her declaration.

"I'm sorry I didn't ask you to explain," she said. "You're an honorable man, Ryan, and you would have never done something like that. It's my fault." She looked down, too ashamed to admit that she hadn't trusted in her own ability to be loved.

"What did you think when you saw that scene?"

She sighed and pulled her hair behind her ears, then clasped her arms around her waist. "I thought what I've always thought. That you couldn't possibly be interested in someone like me."

He pulled her against him. Their faces were so close she could see the dark flecks in his eyes.

"I love you, Faith." His breath was a warm whisper of promise against her lips.

She hadn't expected to hear him say it. Her heart clenched. "You don't have to say that just because—"

He touched his fingers to her lips. "Listen to me. Look at my face. Believe me. I love you."

She listened. She looked. And she believed.

Then she cried. He held her tenderly as she let loose the emotion. Cried because she did believe him, because she'd finally gotten what she'd waited for her entire life.

"I didn't think I was capable of loving anyone until I met you," he said quietly, softly stroking her back.

Faith wiped the tears with the sleeve of her dress. "I didn't think I was worthy of love, until you loved me."

He leaned back and shook his head, laughing. "What a pair we are. Two miserably lonely people, trying to be impersonal about a marriage, and both of us made it as personal as it could get."

Then he swept her into his arms and pressed a long, gloriously passionate kiss on her lips. Faith sighed into his open mouth, their breath mingling in a mixture of love and desire.

"Let's go home, wife. I want to get in bed with the woman I love."

"It's seven in the morning, Ryan," she said with a smile.

He grinned and cocked an eyebrow. "That just gives us more time, doesn't it?"

She threaded her arm through his and strolled from the office.

"I guess in a few months you'll have to find someone to replace me at work," she said as they headed down the hall.

"A few months? How about now?"

Faith laughed. "I think I'll stay on for awhile. I have to keep my eye on you."

He turned toward her and arched a brow. "Me? Why?"

She stopped and threaded her fingers through his hair. "Rich, gorgeous, successful CEO? You're a prime candidate for all the gold diggers out there."

"You worried about my fidelity?"

"Nope." What a wonderful feeling it was to know that, to be certain of a man's love. She never thought she'd experience it in her lifetime, especially with someone like Ryan. But she did feel it.

"Good." As they waited for the elevators he slid his arms around her waist and pulled her against him. She felt his heat and desire and counted the minutes until they could make love again.

When his hands crept down to squeeze her buttocks, she yelped. "Mr. McKay!" she protested in mock horror. "Isn't that a bit personal?"

With a wicked grin he murmured against her lips. "Damn right it is. Get used to it." Then he claimed her mouth and got very, very personal.

Just the way she liked it.

About the Author

Jaci Burton is a Diva who writes in her pajamas, lives on M&Ms and Oreo cookies yet never gains weight. She watches Dr. Phil and Oprah, which is where she gets most of her story ideas. She's married to Charlie, her love slave, who fans her and feeds her grapes when she's too stressed to write. She lives in a castle in the mountainous region of Carpathia, surrounded by gorgeous vampires and werewolves who cater to her every whim. Monstrous killer weredogs protect her realm and prevent other jealous authors from approaching her.

In reality, Jaci lives in Oklahoma with her husband Charlie, her daughter Ashley and five dogs. She does sometimes write in her pajamas, does love M&Ms and Oreo cookies, which sadly will attach themselves to her thighs and butt if she isn't careful. She has been lucky enough to be able to do what she loves most, which is write romance.

You can visit with Jaci at www.jaciburton.com or email her at jaci@jaciburton.com.

Love can rescue a lonely heart.

Rescue Me
© *2006 Jaci Burton*

Kyle Morgan doesn't want to be rescued, especially not by former beauty queen Sabrina Daniels. Sabrina fires up Kyle's long-dormant libido, and it's like a match struck on dry tinder – an explosion of heat whenever she's around. His cheating ex-wife left a bad taste in his mouth about the entire female gender and he doesn't want to get involved again, despite Sabrina's untapped sensuality.

Sabrina Daniels, newly divorced from her controlling millionaire husband, is out to build her independence and begin a new life.

She's always wanted to be a ranch owner but knows nothing about ranching. Her solution comes in the form of The Rocking M in Dreamwater, Oklahoma. The ranch needs an investor, and she has the money. But if she wants her dreams to come true, Sabrina will have to work alongside handsome-as-sin Kyle Morgan. Yes, he's surly and unpleasant, but underneath his tough exterior, she discovers a man who feels like a failure.

Both have firm goals for their future, but love has a way of interfering in the best laid plans.

Available now in ebook and print from Samhain Publishing.

Enjoy the following excerpt from Rescue Me...

"I'm here to rescue you."

Kyle Morgan was so intent on what he was doing he thought the female voice above him was his sister Jenna, bugging him about coming in for lunch.

"I don't need rescuing right now. Get lost." Another turn of the wrench and he might actually be able to get the blasted oil pan loosened.

"That's not what this paper says."

Definitely not his sister's voice. Those weren't Jenna's legs either. But then he couldn't see much while lying in the dirt under the truck. He tilted his head sideways and saw red-painted toenails and slim, tanned ankles. Jenna wouldn't be caught dead in skimpy sandals like that. Definitely *not* his sister.

He slid out from underneath the truck and squinted in the midday sun to see who thought he needed rescuing. All he could make out was a vague shadow attached to very shapely legs.

"Are you going to lie there and stare at me all day?" Her voice was deep and sexy, like skinny-dipping at midnight. Risky, forbidden, yet irresistibly appealing.

He so didn't have time for this. But he was damn curious and needed a break anyway, so he grabbed his shirt off the hood of the old blue Chevy truck, wiping his hands and sweat-soaked, dirty face. Blinking to clear the sunspots out of his eyes, Kyle got his first look at the woman attached to the voice.

Stunning, was his first thought as he gazed at her beautiful face. Golden blonde hair hung in cascading waves over her shoulders and rested just above her full, high breasts. Eyes the color of amber ale stared levelly at him as she licked her lips nervously.

"Are you Kyle Morgan?"

I don't know. Am I? He seemed unable to think about anything except the vision standing in front of him. "I guess I am." *Great answer, dumbass. Sunstroke, obviously. Normally he had a freakin' brain cell.*

"Then as I said before, I'm here to rescue you." A smile that could light up the entire state of Oklahoma graced her face as she held out her hand. "I'm Sabrina Daniels."

Kyle was dimly aware of her slim, warm hand in his as she shook it with fervor. Her skin was soft, like sliding his hand over silk sheets, making him wish he'd had a chance to wash the grime off his.

Suddenly the name sparked recognition. "You're Sabrina Daniels?" Shit. He sure hoped he heard that wrong.

She nodded enthusiastically. "Yes. I'm so glad to finally meet you, Kyle."

So this was the woman who was going to spend the next three months at the Rocking M Ranch. Three months, and he would have to work closely with her every day. He stifled a groan as his eyes washed over her cover-model looks and centerfold body, trying not to lick his lips at the way the blue silk dress hugged her womanly curves. Surely this woman was punishment for something bad he'd done in the past.

Maybe he should have asked for a picture first. She looked totally out of place and too damned distracting. Not good.

"I didn't expect you until tomorrow." Frankly he didn't expect her to show up at all. *Hoped* she wouldn't show was more like it.

"I know. I arrived this morning and thought about grabbing a hotel and waiting until tomorrow but I was so excited I decided to come out a day early. I didn't think you'd mind since we had an agreement and you were expecting me. You were expecting me right?"

The woman waved her hands around as fast as she was talking. He was already getting a headache and watching her swat invisible flies in the air was making him dizzy to boot.

"At first I planned to call, and then I thought if I called you might not let me come today and I really wanted to, so I decided to just show up and throw myself at you and here I am." She inhaled a huge breath of air.

Trying hard to recall if he'd had any whiskey for breakfast that could possibly be screwing with his clarity, he remembered he'd had coffee. So the reason for his confusion had to be the five-foot-six fast-talking tornado standing in front of him.

"Yes I can see you're here." She might be here, but he'd be damned if he was going to be pleasant. No matter how good-looking she was, or how her voice reminded him of sex and sin, or how her face showed the enthusiasm of a child. This wasn't his idea in the first place. "So now what?"

She tilted her head, showing off a creamy expanse of slender neck. Kyle inhaled sharply, trying to avoid thinking of her as a beautiful, desirable woman. He wanted to think of her as a nuisance. Which she was going to be for the next three months.

"Well, now I guess we can get started."

"Get started with what?" He must have had whiskey *with* his coffee this morning.

Sabrina smiled shyly. "With my training."

His thoughts strayed to the kind of training he'd like to give Sabrina Daniels. Damned if all the blood in his brain hadn't migrated toward baser pastures. His long-dormant sex drive sure picked a fine time to spring to life again. Great—now he could add lack of sex to his already long list of frustrations.

Maybe if he thought about all the negative things her presence represented he could get his mind off the fact Sabrina Daniels was a damned attractive woman.

It wasn't working. His mind continued on its wayward sexual course, heating his blood and tightening the crotch of his jeans. Maybe it was the weather. It was damn hot outside, way too hot for late April. He was dirty and sweaty and felt like a pig while she looked fresh and clean and smelled like peaches. He shuddered to think what he must smell like, but it was probably closer to rotted fruit.

He looked her over from head to toe. She crossed her arms across her chest, obviously uncomfortable with his scrutiny. Good. "I hardly think you're dressed to begin anything, other than maybe hosting a cocktail party. And gee, you just missed the one we hosted last night. All the Dreamwater elite were here."

Sarcasm obviously wasn't lost on her as she tapped her sandaled foot in annoyance. Maybe she'd be so irritated she'd leave. He should be so lucky.

"Kyle. I'm hot, I'm thirsty, and I've driven a long way today. It's my understanding we had an agreement and you were expecting me. But if there's a problem with our contract we can discuss it. Is there some place out of the sun we could sit and talk?"

Well hell. If his mother were still alive she'd kick his ass for lack of manners. He finally noticed sheens of perspiration moistened her face, and the shadow between her breasts that kept drawing his eye was damp. She looked about ready to pass out.

"Sorry. Let's go inside where it's cooler."

She nodded gratefully and Kyle directed her toward the large brick ranch house, following behind her. Watching her perfect backside swaying as she walked, it became quite clear this bargain he and his family had struck was a huge mistake.

Kyle didn't want to do business with Sabrina Daniels, but couldn't pinpoint exactly why. Maybe it was the instant attraction he felt for her, bringing to life feelings long held in check. More likely it was because she now held a financial interest in his family's ranch. That meant an outsider owned a part of the Rocking M.

When his parents died and he and his younger brother and sister took over the Rocking M, they vowed the Morgans would retain ownership. And despite everything they'd been through, that's the way it had remained. Until now. Now Sabrina Daniels owned a portion of their ranch. At least temporarily.

If they didn't need the money so damn bad, if he hadn't been forced to pay his cheating ex-wife all that cash in the divorce settlement, they wouldn't be in this predicament now. This was his fault and an investor was the only way to dig the Rocking M out of the deep financial hole he'd put it in.

The sooner he finished his business with Sabrina Daniels and got her off the Rocking M, the happier he'd be. No one was ever going to own this ranch but a Morgan.

GREAT
CHEAP
FUN

Discover eBooks!
THE FASTEST WAY TO GET THE HOTTEST NAMES

Get your favorite authors on your favorite reader, long before they're out in print! Ebooks from Samhain go wherever you go, and work with whatever you carry—Palm, PDF, Mobi, and more.